D0150293

ON ISLAND

Life Among the Coast Dwellers

PAT CARNEY

TOUCHWOODEDITIONS.COM

TouchWood Editions
touchwoodeditions.com

LIBRARY AND ARCHIVES CANADA CATALOGUING IN PUBLICATION
Carney, Patricia, 1935–, author
On island : life among the coast dwellers / Pat Carney.

Short stories.
Issued in print and electronic formats.
ISBN 978-1-77151-210-7 (softcover).

I. Title.

PS8605.A7515O52 2017   C813'.6   C2017-900122-1

Edited by Renée Layberry
Illustrations by Bev Byerley
Design by Pete Kohut

We acknowledge the financial support of the Government of Canada through the Canada Book Fund (CBF) and the Canada Council for the Arts, and of the province of British Columbia through the British Columbia Arts Council and the Book Publishing Tax Credit.

PRINTED IN CANADA AT FRIESENS

18 19 20 21 22   5 4 3

To the people of the coast,
with admiration and affection

CONTENTS

Many of the events in these stories happened somewhere, sometime, on British Columbia's coast. The characters are fictional. Since there are no names, no names have been changed.

Who, where, and when? It is the reader's choice.

Pat Carney
Saturna Island, BC

CAT DUMP

ONE SUNNY SUMMER MORNING A woman drove off the inter-island ferry in her battered white 1986 Saab 900 and parked in front of the Wharf Store, leaving the engine running. Who she was and where she came from doesn't matter. We never see or hear from her again. It is what she did that counts.

In the time it took the ferry crew to discharge the ship's load of cars and passengers and board the traffic heading off island—maybe ten minutes—the woman opened the back-seat door of her car, unloaded a couple of cat carriers, opened their doors and dumped eight cats on the potholed blacktop road. Then she climbed into her car, shifted into gear and drove back on the ferry. She never looked back.

The eight cats staggered to their feet and looked around. They arched their backs to stretch, or sat down and licked their coats or groomed their whiskers, ignoring the glances of the embarking foot passengers. They were a motley mix of felines: tabby, golden, black, grey, black and grey, calico, tortoiseshell and one startlingly beautiful white cat with chocolate ears and blue eyes who glanced calmly about her. They were all very thin.

After the ferry sailed with the woman on board, the wharf area sank back into the singing silence, broken only by the shrieks of the gulls and the intermittent comings and goings of people entering the Wharf Store or the pub built below it.

At first, the cats stayed in the sun-warmed patch of road, guarded only by the cormorants that stood like solitary sentinels, each assigned to the top of a single wooden pile of the island dock. Some cats curled up in the sunlight and slept. Later, as the afternoon shadows cooled the blacktop, they dispersed, one by one, into the bushes or trotting tail up along the edge of the road. By evening, all had disappeared.

The next morning the Professor and his wife, newcomers to island life, were enjoying their fresh brewed morning coffee on the patio of their waterside home. "Look," said the wife excitedly, pointing to the birdbath at the edge of the patio where a young raccoon was standing on its hind legs drinking the rainwater out of the bowl. When it had finished, the raccoon dropped back onto all four feet and moved toward the house. They watched in horror as it vanished into a hole in the basement foundation.

"How will we get it out?" asked the Professor's wife in dismay. She had heard stories of raccoons taking over basements, nesting with their young, chittering away at all hours of the night, entering houses through the cat door in search of food and water, making enormous and foul-smelling messes for the occupants to clean up.

Then, as if on cue, they saw a beautiful white cat with chocolate ears step out of the garden hedge and follow the grey raccoon into the basement through the hole in the foundation. They held their breath, waiting for the carnage, the tearing of flesh, the screams of pain from the little cat that was sure to follow when the raccoon turned on the invader.

Instead, there was silence. The couple picked up their coffee mugs and retreated into the house, shutting the glass patio door firmly behind them. Island life was not for the faint of heart.

Later that day, the Church Warden phoned his wife on her cell phone from his cluttered workshop attached to his garage. She was playing bridge in the Community Hall.

"What is it?" she asked irritably, studying her hand.

"I am being held hostage by a cat," he said in a voice pitched low to avoid being overheard by the tabby that crouched at the workshop door with baleful eyes, barring his exit.

"That's ridiculous," his wife snapped. She surprised herself. It was uncharacteristic of her to speak so sharply to her overbearing husband. "You can't be serious."

"But it won't let me leave the workshop," he replied gruffly, eyeing the cat. "It moves when I do and blocks my way." He didn't like cats. They were one species he couldn't intimidate.

"It's probably hungry," said his wife impatiently. Her bridge partners were listening intently to her side of the conversation. "Take a can of tuna from the earthquake supplies cupboard in the garage, open it, put it down beside the cat, and then step over it."

The Church Warden did what she ordered. He was able to retreat to their house beyond the garage, where he poured himself a rum and Coke. The next morning, he found the tabby sitting on the back step off the kitchen, paws tucked under its body, eyes fixed on the kitchen door.

The Church Warden sighed. "Let's call it a truce," he told the cat, turning away to write cat food on the shopping list on the refrigerator door.

A day or two later, the Master Gardener was examining his climbing beans in the community garden down in the valley when he noticed a black and grey cat crouched in the long grass near the Cat House, the penned enclave where the islanders nurtured the abandoned strays and feral cats they collected from all over the island.

The present Cat House population was nine, all housed in gaily decorated boxes and kennels retrieved from the Free Store at the Recycling Centre. Although clearly fatigued but too proud to beg for food, the black and grey cat exuded a certain male authority from his post in the grass. The Master Gardener calculated the number of males and females, all spayed or neutered—or "fixed," in island parlance—currently in residence and concluded there was room for one more.

"Why do people who move off island think their pets can survive on their own and leave them to fend for themselves?" the Gardener muttered to his plants. "Indoor cats aren't mousers. And they can't defend themselves from mink or raccoons."

He approached the cat in the grass slowly, with a soft step. The cat quickly retreated. A crow perched in the trees along the road cawed a caution. The Gardener thought. He couldn't leave the gate to the Cat House open or the resident cats might escape.

He crossed the street to his garage where he stored his cat food, opened a can of whitefish, and spooned some into a cat dish. He poured fresh water into another container. He went back to the Cat House, placed the food and water near the gate, and left the garden.

That evening, when he went back to feed the resident cats, the dish near the gate was empty. There was no sign of the black and grey cat in the grass. It might take a few days, thought the Gardener, but eventually he would coax the visitor into the Cat House to join the others. Unless a mink got to him first.

Goldie the golden retriever rescued the golden cat in the Dog Patch up the road by the island's only General

Store, where shoppers were encouraged to tie their dogs to the trees to reduce the risk of them being run over by the island vehicles that rumbled in and out of the narrow parking lot. Goldie's owner, a musician known as Blondie, was collecting the mail at the island Post Office, located inside the General Store.

She also picked up a bottle of Little Creek salad dressing to assist the local sheep farmer, who fitted the empty bottles with special screw-on lamb nipples, made in New Zealand, and recycled them as lambing aids to supply the baby lambs with extra milk.

She stopped for a coffee in the adjacent café, snatching a quick read from the *Guardian* newspaper on the communal table by the serve-yourself coffee flasks on the counter. The café was staffed on a complicated schedule dictated by ferry schedules and recycling hours that brought customers in for a gossip and the cinnamon buns and a few food items, although most islanders did their big shop on their weekly trip to town on Big Island. Seniors on OAP, or old-age pension, travelled on days when pedestrian fares were reduced.

When the musician came out of the café and walked over to the Dog Patch she found a tail-wagging Goldie with a small golden cat in its mouth. "What have you got *this* time?" she asked the dog, who responded with more frantic tail wagging, unable to bark an answer with his mouth full of golden fur.

The musician and her partner lived up the mountain that

centred the island and provided refuge and pasture for the herd of feral goats that overran the higher meadows. Over time, the couple collected abandoned and orphaned animals until they could find homes for them.

The musician gently detached the golden furball from the dog's mouth and determined it was a cat, not much more than a kitten. To her surprise, the little cat was purring. Her heart was thumping through the chest of her thin body as the musician held it in her long-fingered hands.

The musician carefully placed the golden cat in her shopping basket and placed it in the front seat of her Jeep, away from the enthusiastic attentions of her dog, now in the back seat. I do not need another cat, she thought as she started the Jeep and headed out of the parking lot. We already have two outside mousers. But I can't leave it in the Dog Patch. She turned onto the one-lane gravel road that led up the mountain, the cat purring in the basket on the seat beside her.

A few nights later two islanders left the island's only pub at closing time, their bellies full of beer, lurched up the stairs linking the pub to the road, and climbed into an ancient Ford Ranger pickup. The driver put it in gear, backed the truck up, and swung it around to turn onto the main road.

It was dark as Satan. There were no street lights. The evening ferry had come and gone, discharging its grumpy load of shoppers returning from scrounging Seniors Day bargains in town. The driver and his passenger had no fear of police roadblocks as the pickup made its noisy and erratic way up the hill from the ferry. There were no police stationed on the island.

They ran over the black cat as it scurried across the road from the Community Hall, where it had taken refuge with a grey companion cat after being dumped in front of the store. The Hall was skirted with cedar boards, some of which were missing, giving the building a toothless appearance but also offering protection from the rain to stray animals.

The driver and his passenger felt the soft squish as the tire ran over the black cat. The driver braked to a stop. The men tumbled out of the pickup and stared at the dead body of the animal splayed over the blacktop under the front left tire. The passenger swore. "What do we do with it?" he asked his buddy. "We can't just leave this mess here for the morning walk-on ferry passengers to trip over."

"I dunno," said the driver. His beer-sloshed brain was trying to focus on the dead black animal lying under the tire. It was so dark it was hard to see anything beyond its shape, humping up from the blacktop.

"Maybe if we lay it in the Church Warden's driveway he can see it gets buried," offered the passenger. He didn't know whether to burp or throw up.

"Right on," said the driver.

They retrieved a shovel from the bed of the pickup and scooped up the cat's broken body and drove to the Warden's house beside the church. They carefully laid the dead cat at the entrance to the driveway on the ridge in the centre so that the Warden would be sure to see it.

Except, of course, it was the Church Warden's wife who discovered the dead cat, laid out so straight in the middle of the driveway, when she went out for her morning walk. Shocked and upset, she ran back to her house shrieking for her husband, who was dumping kibble into a dish for his newly adopted tabby. He left it to nibble away while he soothed his wife and figured out where to bury the dead cat. The tabby didn't look up from its dish.

The grey cat, who had observed the squishy demise of the black cat, decided to take up residence behind the cedar skirts of the Community Hall, earning his keep on mouse patrol in the community kitchen, endearing himself to islanders as the official caretaker and community cat, rarely missing a concert or a public meeting and showing up for regular yoga classes.

The off-islander was adopted by the calico cat that was living in the pub's outside eating area that accommodated families who wanted coffee and food but couldn't take their young children into the pub's licensed premises. His wife and two children were eating their lamb burgers and chips at the tables in the garden when a child noticed the pretty calico cat, with its orange and white coat and black eye patch, sitting by his feet under the planked table, gazing fixedly at the burger in his hand.

The cat was down to skin and bones, its ribs protruding through its fur. It was clearly starving. "Oh please, Mommy, can't we take it home?" the children cried.

Mommy looked at Daddy, who shrugged his shoulders. He wouldn't be the one feeding it and changing the litter box. The parents asked the bartender for a box and some newspapers, and the family, plus cat, packed up and drove onto the ferry.

No one ever rescued the tortoiseshell cat. Nobody remembered what it looked like. It simply disappeared into the forest. Maybe it died. Maybe the wolf killed it. Maybe it found a feral family of cats and lived happily ever after.

Who knows?

NATURE LOVERS

WHEN THE COUPLE FIRST CAME to the island, they experienced the initial stage of adapting to island lifestyle: euphoria. They rhapsodized over the beauty of the sea, the green forests marching up and over the island's mountain backbone, the friendly people in their unpretentious homes, the home-grown veggies for sale at absurdly low prices at the Saturday village outdoor market, the prawn boat tied up at the dock when the fishery was open. Time was measured by the rise and fall of the tides, the coming and going of the ferries.

Bliss, they told each other fondly, secretly pleased their spouse shared their pleasure.

It was her idea to move to the island after he retired from his law practice in town. Every business day of his working life he opened the files on his desk, dealing with the marital debris of divorce, partner disputes over the roadkill of their bankrupt businesses, drunk-driving charges facing people protesting their innocence.

"Every day I deal with somebody's disaster," he often complained to her. "Is this all there is?" He sighed, not expecting her to answer, and retired to his study with his newspaper folded open at the Sudoku puzzle.

His solace was his appointment as an adjunct Professor of Law at the University, where he tried, with some success, to expose his students to the seedy realities of the careers they had chosen beyond the expectation of a fat income. He took to referring to himself as Professor.

When he came into a modest inheritance, he sold the practice to his partner with great relief and retired, with more regret, from the university law faculty.

Rejuvenated, the couple assessed the opportunities that might be available and practical for their senior years. He thought of buying a bankrupt pub up-island. But despite her small-town background, she couldn't see herself as a publican's wife.

He mused on returning to his roots upcountry, with its sage-spiked hills fringed with timber, and nostalgically recalled his early adolescence on an orchard above green Okanagan Lake, boring their daughter with tales of his victories over raccoons stealing the ripened fruit and his battles with armies of tent caterpillars.

But his wife didn't like her in-laws, who were openly dismayed when he married a social worker from an Interior town after the expense they incurred sending him to law school in the city, with its rich sorority girls looking for their MRS degree.

And so, when she found the real estate advertisement about the cottage by the sea, she booked the ferry to the island on a summer day of blue skies, warm sun, and calm seas. She thought they were in an earthly Paradise, protected by a national park that annexed part of the islands in the Salish Sea. They were happily ensconced in their cottage within a few weeks.

By winter, they entered the second phase of adapting to the island lifestyle: alarm. Winter brought storms, dark skies, endless rain. The power went out for days, the ferries were cancelled, the veggies in the only island store grew pale and limp, the villagers hibernated in their tree-shrouded houses. No birdsong or children's voices on the beach. Only silence. Deafening, pervasive stillness, broken only by sporadic squalls of wind thrashing the suddenly threatening trees.

"Why did you bring us to this godforsaken rock?" cried the husband accusingly, pointing his finger at his wife. "What have you done with our lives?"

His wife put another chunk of cedar in the wood stove. She had no answer, because she had no idea.

By the following spring they had lapsed into the third phase: acceptance. "Making the best of it," they affirmed to each other. Their only daughter had flown the nest and was busily building her own life up the coast. And the sea view cottage, they told each other, was very comfortable and affordable, despite the outrageous taxes.

When the beautiful white cat with the chocolate ears moved in with them they felt their island family was complete.

So the couple tried to fit in. They bought Symphony tickets for Sunday concerts in town on the Big Island. They went to the monthly Women's Club dinners, joined the local service club, played bridge on Wednesday afternoons, and enjoyed the concerts in the Community Hall. They also attended the island's only church.

She joined the book club, although nobody ever seemed to have read the assigned books. Instead, members hotly debated the salacious details of island marital breakdown, gay and straight—they were liberal minded, they told each other.

They wanted to avoid being considered a "blow-in," as her new friend, the Church Warden's wife, called the Come-From-Away crowd—the part-time islanders who wintered in their RVs in some Arizona mobile home park and returned in the spring sporting their desert tans. Although the couple headed for the sun in January, as did every other island resident with bus fare to escape south, spending two weeks in Kauai at a bed and breakfast a few blocks from the beach.

She didn't demur when he suggested opening a shop down by the ferry landing, selling antiquarian and second-hand books, sheet music, local art, and even antiques mined from the furniture shops that littered the Big Island highways.

But the shop was not a success. He bought a great many books during his forays, but nothing on his shelves seemed to be for sale. He preferred talking to potential customers than marketing his products. The customers, in turn, were not much interested in acquiring the entire collection of Patricia Cornwall murder mysteries or Dick Francis stories.

With the exception of the odd musician, few people were interested in old sheet music anymore. And well-priced second-hand furniture couldn't compete with free items from the Recycling Centre across from the medical clinic.

But the Professor was a great raconteur, with a host of stories from his law practice about human foibles and people's misbehaviour, and an audience willing to listen. Even the two visiting tax collectors from Ottawa, who were checking out the mystifying failure of island businesses to file annual tax returns, left his shop with a complimentary book on hiking trails but little information on bookshop revenues.

Fitting in also included participating in the many activities offered by the marine environment. But she couldn't manage a kayak, given her arthritis, and he was never a fisherman. He was a freshwater boater, accustomed to upcountry lakes and rivers, secretly afraid of the pull and churn of tides. His one attempt to run a second-hand powerboat ended when the ancient engine quit and he had to paddle the unruly sixteen-foot aluminum boat back to the government dock.

Still in pursuit of outdoor activities, the couple examined the nature walks that threaded the island's valleys and ridges.

When spring rains melted the last vestiges of snow, they decided to tackle one of the easier trails that wound from the gravel road along the creek through flat terrain to the bottom of the waterfall that fell down the mountain from the creek's source above.

They parked the car by the roadside, put on their ponchos, picked up their walking sticks and headed down the trail through the ferns and cedars, breathing in the chilled air. It restores our souls, she thought, planting her stick in the weeds that edged the trail. It was a grey day, with the smell of rain.

The trail grew muddy. Water filled the tire tracks that rutted the path. The Professor swung down the trail, sloshing through the silt in his high rubber boots. Behind him his wife, more modestly shod in rubber slip-ons, stepped on the ridge between the tire tracks, swung her other leg forward, and sank into a sludge-filled pothole. She straddled the trail, her arms stretched sideways for balance, until she retrieved her right leg with a sucking noise and wobbled forward.

She was desperately afraid she would fall and lie in the mud like a great green slug, unable to pick herself up. There was no sign of her husband, who had disappeared around the corner through the branches. A songbird chirped derisively, *stupid, stupid, stupid*. She could hear the sound of someone hammering in the valley behind her, probably a volunteer building plant beds in the community garden near the baseball field.

Would he hear her screams? Above her a woodpecker knocked his brains out on the trunk of a young hemlock. We are doing the same, she thought.

She staggered through the silt, trying to keep to the higher ground at the edge of the trail, until she turned the corner and encountered her husband, mired in the mud, only the tops of his boots showing above the water. He was immobilized, like a tall fishing heron standing on stalk legs.

Wordlessly she stuck out her walking stick to give him leverage. He grasped it and she slowly turned him around, pulling his boots out of the silt, towing him back toward her. They slogged their way back to the car in silence.

They never made it to the waterfall in the woods.

The Professor retired to his books and Sudoku puzzles. His wife gamely pressed on. She joined an Oyster Walk planned by the Park Guide to search for the mysterious native oyster—with its small, cupped shell instead of the larger, flatter Pacific species Europeans introduced—that the island's Aboriginal people had harvested in the past.

The day of the walk was dark and drizzly with a surly sea. The beach revealed one of the lowest tides of the year. But after an hour she abandoned the motley group of tourists in their T-shirts and short pants and flip-flops, stranded on the uneven stones and tidal mud slippery with wet kelp, afraid she would twist her ankle, or worse. Later she learned from the Park Guide that no native oysters were found.

She skipped the Park's advertised Activity Day examination of owl pellets, a popular event attracting leggy children who whooped through the forest exploring for clues about what owls ate by poking sticks at their pellets scattered on the forest floor.

The Berry Bonanza walk was more appetizing. She was beginning to get the hang of a nature lover's apparel, and arrived wearing sturdy shoes, a floppy green hat, and a rain jacket, with a walking stick in hand and a small notebook and pen stuffed in a pocket.

As they hiked down the paths away from the Aboriginal middens, the Park Guide shrilled the usual admonition, "Don't pick the berries—look, but don't touch," while she hunted for culprits whose chins were smeared with evidence of consuming the forbidden salal berries and wild blueberries harvested from the abundant bushes lining the path.

Discouraged, secretly afraid she would never fit in with the ebb and flow of island life, she read the poster on the General Store door announcing a guided walk in the Park for novice birdwatchers. Bravely, she signed up.

It was a cloudy, sun-spattered morning when the island birdwatchers gathered in the gravel parking lot near the beach at the appointed time.

The group included the Park Guide, in her official green shorts and khaki shirt and Smoky the Bear hat, the lanky island amateur bird expert, and a gaggle of islanders, dressed in flip-flops and boots and shorts and outdoor gear, cameras swinging from their necks. Some wore headgear as protection against encounters with nettles, scratchy bushes and tree branches. The wife adjusted her floppy hat.

The island expert scratched his lean legs and gave a short talk on what birds they were likely to see. The Park Guide pulled her Blackberry device from her pocket and played some recorded bird calls they were likely to hear.

The group moved down the trail, while they discussed what the bird calls in the forest around them sounded like.

"That one is saying, 'cheeseburger, cheeseburger,'" said one woman, her hair pulled back in a ponytail. "But I can't remember its name."

A man wearing a Tilley hat loosely fastened below his Adam's apple announced, "That's an Olive-sided flycatcher. It is saying, 'free beer, free beer.'"

A senior, squinting through his spectacles and leaning on his stick said, "That call sounds like someone hailing a taxi from the curb in town."

The wife realized that the only sounds her city-raised colleagues could relate to were urban ones. They rarely heard the melodies sung by birds in the countryside.

The island expert instructed, "The American robin and the western tanager sound alike. See if you can tell the difference." The group cocked their collective ears and listened. There was a deep drone. "That's a Beaver," said the island expert, pointing to a small float plane skipping like a dragonfly over the water.

"A bird of sorts," said the bespectacled senior dryly.

A house finch trilled from the top of a tree in the parking lot. The Park Guide said the birdwatchers would likely hear the common yellowthroat, and a Wilson's warbler. What they mostly heard was the gargling and gabbing of Canada geese.

"Sounds like barking dogs penned in a backyard," said a teenager derisively, who clearly would rather be at the cabin playing video games instead of being dragged outdoors by his parents.

The group set off single file down the Park's new gravel path, which replaced the old woodland path down by the water, deemed by the culturally sensitive bureaucrats as located too near the Aboriginal middens for access by the public. The *crunch*, *crunch* of hiking boots over the gravel obliterated any bird sounds.

When they stopped at the sound of a bird call, people tilted their head and adopted the glazed expression of birdwatchers everywhere. They listened for the "teet" of a Pacific-slope flycatcher. Or the trill of a thrush. "The First Nations call the thrush a salmonberry bird because it trills when salmonberries are out," said the Park Guide as the group approached a marshy area of willows and bulrushes.

They heard "beet beet." "Nuthatch," said one person with a French accent. "It sounds like a truck backing up." They heard a varied thrush. "Sounds like a cell phone," said the teenager.

A blackbird, which could actually be seen in a hawthorn

bush beside the path, called *cheap, cheap*. As different bird calls broke the morning silence the group argued over the source of the sounds. Wilson's warbler! Chickadee! Robin! In the sky above a vulture with huge V-shaped wings circled the marsh where the group debated amiably among themselves.

They clanged their way over the metal-meshed boardwalk that edged the marsh. There was a great warbling crescendo of melodious sound. "Warblers," said the wife, delighted. She never remembered the names of the birds and could never hear anything over the caw of the crows, the barking of the geese.

"Frogs," said everybody else. The frogs created a wave of sound that then died away as the watchers stared at the still, stagnant brown waters of the marsh. Birds flitted over the bulrushes. Bees and insects hummed in the marsh like city traffic heard at a distance.

They returned to the gravel path, covered in needles and fallen leaves, and headed down to the beach, pebbled with stones and oyster shells, at a safe distance from the middens, and listened to the squabbling of the gulls. A heron fished from the point of land that curved into the Gulf. Offshore, a kayak glided by, a limp windsock hanging from a mast rigged in the bow.

A powerboat zigzagged expertly through the pass between the island and a rocky reef. The driver obviously knew where the hidden rock, which smashed so many island propellers, lay underwater below the clashing currents.

Pointing to the black birds lined up on the reef, the island expert described the sloppy dives of cormorants. "They stand so straight backed, but when they fly and dive to land on the water, it looks like a disaster is going to happen," he said.

Someone kicked at a rock where past visitors had painted graffiti, which was gradually being eroded by the tides. The birdwatchers looked at a black oystercatcher walking along the beach, fishing for food at the tide line. It was a large, black shorebird with a reddish beak and orange feet. "When I see someone walking in town with orange clogs, I say, 'You are wearing oystercatchers,'" said the woman with the ponytail, smiling.

The wife sat gratefully on a bench, breathing in the cool, fresh breeze from the sea, and observed the scene before her. The rocks below the bench were robed in seaweed, sequined with barnacles, tasseled with kelp bulbs floating on the silky sea.

The urban touchstones of a walk in the wilderness, she thought, rising from the bench and joining the group headed for breakfast and coffee at the island's café.

She was fitting in with the best of them. Maybe she might become an islander herself. One day.

PRIESTS AND PAGANS

THE CHURCH WARDEN NOTICED THE church sign was missing when he was on his weekly mouse patrol. The sign stood on the church grounds at the juncture of the island's two main gravel roads. It proclaimed the church to be Anglican, but there was no other church on island, so it was known simply as the Church.

Now the sign was missing. The wooden stand that framed it stood empty, the chains swinging aimlessly in the sea breeze. Kids, thought the Warden. Damn island kids again, not enough to do except vandalize private property.

The Church Warden was a large man, with the complacent countenance of a cream-fed cat, and he took his duties seriously. A retired forestry engineer, he favoured long-term solutions, consistent with his experience in planning logging roads for forests that would be harvested years later.

He normally wore khaki pants and shirts from the Three

Vets Army Surplus Store and selected his shoes from the Free Store at the Recycling Centre, snaring a spiffy set of oxfords when the local doctor died. On Remembrance Day and other special occasions, he wore a white shirt, a navy blazer, and slacks that he believed to be grey but were actually a greenish tint; he was colour blind.

His only real vice was a fondness for Copenhagen chewing tobacco, common in his time among men who couldn't smoke on the job in the woods, as he told his wife when she complained about the plugs of tobacco she found in the bathroom sink.

He whacked his cane at the blackberry bushes surrounding the church, looking for the sign. The church itself was built by island pioneers with money scrimped from the Mission Fund, designed to bring religion to the pagans in some foreign land. The island was neither foreign nor pagan, but it was as far from the Mainland as one could be without sailing into American waters half a nautical mile offshore.

The church was built in the form of an upside-down boat. The pioneer builders didn't know how to build a church, but they knew how to build a fishboat. The hand-crafted arches that supported the roof were similar to the ribs cradling a ship's hull. It was named after the patron saint of sailors and those who travel by water.

The islanders had an ambiguous relationship with the church, which was available to all for weddings, funerals, and all-too-occasional baptisms. People who rarely attended services mowed the lawn, cleaned the gutters, replaced the splintered doors, and planted the maple tree in the sunlit clearing in the surrounding forest. The local quilting circle contributed the quilts for the altar.

Islanders sporadically patronized the Fair Trade shop, which the Altar Guild ladies operated in the church basement, where one could buy bamboo salad bowls from Vietnam and colourful African dolls. A cupboard housed a jar of instant coffee, teabags, sugar cubes and creamers, some cups, and an electric kettle for the use of various groups, including local members of Alcoholics Anonymous, and a social justice group that gathered occasionally to discuss spousal abuse and violence against women and valued the anonymity of the shop in an island community of snoops and gossips.

When a new organ was needed, the music fund was oversubscribed by islanders who enjoyed the Christmas carol services. And when the community choir, which sometimes rehearsed in the building, needed a piano, the church's music director found one on Craigslist and had it trucked to the island and tuned.

The church scheduled Holy Communion services twice a month, but in fact it accommodated a variety of religious practices. The retired United Church minister held regular meditation sessions, attended by the local Buddhist. An American theologian who was a part-time resident held occasional interdenominational services, lecturing on popular subjects like "Sin and Scriptures" and "Who Wrote the Bible?" A mildly evangelical pastor held joyful services with songs and prayers and candles.

Not everyone felt comfortable in the wooden pews circled below the large red glass cross, however. Quaker services scheduled for the church were later moved to the plainly decorated Community Hall.

The church sign, decorated with a ship's bell from a sunken American naval ship, proclaimed ALL ARE WELCOME. Who would take issue with that? Obviously someone did, muttered the Warden as he attacked the blackberry bushes.

The assault on the blackberry bushes did not produce any sign. He checked under the porch where the Christmas Nativity scene figures were stored, but his search did not bear fruit. He made a note to call the priest, who resided on another island, and resumed his mouse patrol in the Fair Trade shop in the church basement.

The Church Warden was a confirmed and communicant Anglican, who studied his catechism and ate the wafer and sipped the wine from the cup at Holy Communion services. He had the irritating habit of chanting the prayers slightly in advance of his fellow worshipers. "Our Father who art in Heaven" . . .

"In Heaven . . . ," murmured the others.

"Hallowed be Thy Name . . ."

"Thy Name . . . ," echoed the others.

At least it irritated the priest.

When first appointed to his post by the Bishop, the Church Warden unearthed copies of the Canon Law from the diocesan archives, which set out the responsibilities assigned Church Wardens since the sixteenth century. The main duties listed were to support the priest and control the vermin.

He did his best for the priest but pursued the latter assignment religiously, baiting mousetraps with peanut butter and setting them out on the worn linoleum floor in the church basement each Sunday night, returning to dispose of the dead mice before the Altar Guild ladies turned up on Wednesday to plug in their ancient electric kettle and make their tea.

Returning home after his fruitless search, the Church Warden discussed the sign's mysterious disappearance with his wife, an angular woman with anxious eyes whom he met and married in a mid-coast logging community where she taught elementary school students. Secretly the Warden's wife was relieved; she did not care for the church sign, which had been finished with an orange-tinted varnish, giving it a Halloween-like aspect.

He then phoned the priest, who sounded uninterested and vague. The priest did not allow such earthly matters to distract him from his main interest, the study of scripture. He once told the Warden's wife that he read philosophy at university and turned to the church because it was the only profession that paid him to read. He was currently absorbed in the study of the Gospel of John.

That evening, seated in his reclining chair, sipping his rum and Coke and finishing the crossword puzzle in the newspaper, the Church Warden considered whether the removal of the church sign was a prank of some sort. Putting down his pencil, he told the tabby cat purring on his knee, "Looks like the work of the Devil to me."

His bookish interests centred on conspiracy theories of various kinds, such as exploring the concept that the Apollo 11 moon photo was all a hoax, and he was considerably cheered when a national newspaper columnist reported that Canadian supernova author Margaret Atwood suggested the "One small step for man, one giant leap for mankind" scene may have been filmed in the moon-like mining landscape of the Canadian Shield.

The Church Warden had not actually read Atwood's books—nor, for that matter, the works of any woman author (with the exception of Ayn Rand)—but he made a note to buy any book Atwood wrote that mentioned the possibility of a moon landing misstep.

But when it came to the church's sign, he couldn't think of what anyone would have to gain by removing it. He headed off to bed.

A few weeks later the Church Warden ruminated aloud on the fate of the sign while drinking his ritual strong blend of coffee at the common table in the island café attached to the island's General Store. The island's only grocery store was open in the summer and on winter weekends and Monday afternoons, but closed on Tuesdays except after holiday Mondays. The café was closed on Tuesdays, Wednesdays, and Thursdays, but was open for Friday night pizza and weekends. Off-season sales were slow.

Finally the store clerk, who doubled as the waitress, took pity on him. "I know who took the sign," she said.

"You do?" asked the Warden, slurping his coffee, organically grown in some Third World country and guaranteed to be produced under certified Fair Trade conditions. "Who would do such a thing?"

"The Sunday School teacher," blurted the store clerk. "She said it was demonic, the work of Satan. It contains pagan symbols. She discussed it here in the store with some of the Sunday School mothers and they agreed with her."

"Holy crap!" sputtered the Warden, setting his coffee cup on the table with a rattle. "I mean, holy cow! It's church property! How could she do such a thing?" But the store clerk had returned to more secular issues, restocking the liquor shelves.

The Warden pondered how best to proceed. The small congregation was a mixed lot of believers. Some did not belong to any particular religious denomination but considered themselves Christians. One told the Warden she was a Christian but did not believe in Jesus Christ.

The Sunday School teacher was a good soul who took the religious instruction of her young students, including her own children, very seriously. She was associated with a small section of the congregation who might be classified as evangelical Christians.

To accommodate them, the priest briefly experimented with projecting the Holy Communion service and the hymns on a small screen in front of the altar so that those of the congregation who were moved to do so could wave their arms above their heads when they sang. None were so moved, and the experiment ended.

The priest was inclined toward liturgical dance, swooping around the church bat-like in his black robes for the sombre Good Friday service, dressing in more colourful vestments—gold-trimmed green or white—for the more festive seasons on the church calendar, such as Easter and Christmas. He was a popular member of various theatrical groups on his home island until he had his head shaved for a cancer fundraiser, limiting his potential roles.

The little church had its share of controversy in its short history. Some of the evangelical members of the congregation had charged the previous Reverend Father, a rotund little retired army veteran, with practising heresy in his sermons. They went to the Bishop with their complaint.

The Bishop, a sloth-like man loath to leave his cathedral on the Big Island, called in the Reverend Father and asked him to explain himself.

"I am very upset," said the Reverend Father.

"You should be, provoking your congregation with your preaching," chided the Bishop.

"It's not that," said the Reverend Father. "The problem is that I don't have a white robe to wear when I am burned at the stake."

Nothing more was said about heretical preaching or flame-proof clerical vestments.

After some thought, the Church Warden put the word out that removing (stealing) the sign from the church (private property) was a crime and that he was considering bringing in the RCMP detachment stationed off island. However, if the sign was returned, no further questions would be asked.

Two weeks later, the missing sign was found under the church deck next to the Nativity figures, returned by unknown persons. An examination of the sign by the Warden revealed that the so-called pagan symbols, which had inspired its removal, were tiny carvings that resembled shamrocks.

This distressed the Church Warden's wife, who was Irish. She was named for St. Patrick, the patron saint of Ireland, who in the fifth century preached The Word to the pagan Irish *in ultimis terrae*, or living at the ends of the earth. The analogy was not lost on the wife, who at times suffered the isolation of island living.

Angry accusations flew back and forth among members of the congregation. The Bishop stirred himself to call a church meeting, dispatching a neutral priest from the Big Island since the parish priest was under suspicion of being party to the pagan plot of the orange shamrocks.

The congregation gathered in the small church, seating themselves in the wooden pews in opposing groups, one supporting the Sunday School teacher, while those who sided with the Church Warden settled themselves across the aisle.

The parachuted priest stood between them, reading from the Prayers of the People and pleading for a peaceful resolution. The effect of the orange shamrocks on the Sunday School children was warmly debated.

The Church Warden's wife spoke passionately about St. Patrick and his reputed use of the three-leaf shamrock to signify the Holy Trinity to his pagan Irish parishioners, and then collapsed into her pew in tears, dabbing her eyes with a white linen hankie embossed with a Celtic cross.

It was finally agreed that the sign had been carved by a reformed drunk and non-believer, now deceased, and donated to the church as a gesture of defiance. After coffee and cookies in the church basement, everyone felt better, except the visiting priest, who longed for his own pagan-free parish. At the end of the meeting, members of the congregation went about their business in the spirit of righteousness.

The Warden ordered two new signs for the church grounds. The first, down by the road, had the traditional Anglican Church of Canada symbol. The second, closer to the church, carved in subdued shades of tan and brown and decorated with tiny churches, said, All Are Welcome. No shamrocks graced either sign.

The Sunday School teacher's children outgrew Sunday School, and she left the island to pursue a successful career in local government. The priest was promoted to a red-robed position on the Big Island when the Bishop retired. The new priest became the unit commander of the Coast Guard Auxiliary and spent her spare time, praise the Lord, fishing boaters out of the sea.

The Church Warden read the island children Bible stories after school and turned over the mouse detail to the island chapter of Alcoholics Anonymous to deal with during its weekly meetings.

Each year, when the Santa Claus boat came to the government dock to dispense Christmas presents, the children trooped up the hill to the little church to eat pizza and decorate the Advent Tree in anticipation of the birth of Jesus Christ on Christmas Day.

The work of the Lord, sighed the Warden's wife, with a little help from St. Patrick.

GARDEN PARTY

THE WILD TURKEYS CAME TO the village centre for Thanksgiving weekend. They appeared out of the bushes and walked briskly through the main intersection past the Fire Hall and the General Store, where islanders were picking up their dead domestic turkeys for the holiday dinner. Two wild turkeys hiked along the main road on their long legs, walking on the shoulder, facing traffic, gobbling away to each other like a long-married couple out for an afternoon walk in the late autumn sun.

"Their timing is awkward," observed the Professor's wife, resting on her rake in the community garden as the turkeys strolled by. "Although, in fact, they don't look very appetizing."

"Pretty scrawny," agreed another garlic planter, sipping on some red wine in a plastic cup. Planting garlic and harvesting it the following spring required copious amounts of red wine, juice, salmon dip, and assorted goodies deposited on a weathered, wooden table that teetered unsteadily in the grass near the garden fence, under the supervision of Buster the Garden Dog. He guarded the goodies with his perennial hopeful look on his whiskered face, and harassed the feline inhabitants of the Cat House adjacent to the community garden.

The autumn rains had started, turning the soil squishy and the paths soggy. When the sun came out and the weather turned colder, the Master Gardener summoned the gardeners, who carried shovels, ski poles, hoes, bottles of wine, and bags of goodies to share, to the community garden to plant their garlic.

The garlic planters were a convivial group, bonded by a commitment to their belief that they grew the best garlic on island. They included the editor of the island weekly, the fire chief, the retired Professor and his wife, the schoolteacher and his family, including their newest baby, the café chef, and the Church Warden and his wife, who had told the newcomers about the community garden during bridge sessions in the Community Hall.

Now the gardeners argued amiably over the genesis of the wild turkeys. "Maybe they are escapees from the baker's farm," suggested the fire chief, who knew every property on island.

"No, they were left behind when the couple who were raising llamas loaded their animals onto their truck and left the island on the night ferry, leaving their bills and the poultry behind," said the editor, who knew everything about everybody on island.

"No, they are at least fourth-generation birds that went wild when the original settler died," said the Church Warden, who had lived on island longer than any other member of the garden party.

The turkeys paid no attention to any of them and strutted on down the road toward the beach.

The garlic group all stood like soldiers at their respective raised beds. The Church Warden's wife, shivering in the unseasonal cold, nervously clutched her Nordic pole that she planned to use as her planting instrument. They all listened as the Master Gardener gave his instructions.

First, they should dig up the soil in their boxes and mark grid lines in the earth, about six inches across both ways. The ski poles were perfect for this task.

Second, at the intersections of the lines, they should bore a hole in the soil "exactly" three inches deep. The Church Warden's wife wondered how she should measure this, stabbing the hole with the tip of her Nordic pole after removing its little rubber bootie.

Third, they should select the best, biggest garlic clove (they had been purchased from a Big Island organic grower) and drop it in the hole, pointy tip at the top, and smooth the soil over the sown garlic, and leave it to winter over.

The Master Gardener admonished them not to water

during the first two weeks of May. "That is why you can't plant other crops between the garlic rows," he explained, sticking his hoe deep into the soil of his box, like sheathing his sword. "At least not until you harvest your garlic in late spring."

The garlic group sighed as they gathered at the trestle table to open the wine and drink mugs of hot coffee and munch the cinnamon buns from the island bakery. Spring seemed a long way off, given the gloom of the winter to come, before they could sample the delicious, hot, spicy garlic cloves, the fruit of their labour.

No wonder garlic was the one crop islanders rarely shared with their neighbours. Zucchini, tomatoes, squash, kale, even cabbages were generously divvied up among friends. But not the precious garlic cloves.

One of the joys of island living was the access to locally grown food. Although not abundant, since the island's hummocky geography restricted prime farmland mainly to the valley and the bench of land that supported the sheep farm, islanders grew an amazing amount of veggies and salad greens in their cold frames and small greenhouses and backyard plots in season.

The sheep farm provided grass-fed lamb and beef slaughtered on the property in a government-approved facility, to the envy of residents of other islands not so endowed. Eggs could be purchased from the young biker who lived in an aluminum trailer and nurtured his chicks with loving care normally reserved for young children, cosseting them with garden greens and table scraps contributed by grateful customers.

Some islanders grew their own veggies and sold the surplus in high summer, when their gardens were lush with produce, at the open-air Saturday market held in the gravel parking lot of the General Store. Also on offer were gleaming jars of jelly and jam, dill pickles and pickled beets, apple chutney and antipasto, all produced on island.

Inspired by her neighbours, that first summer the Professor's wife planted lettuce and arugula seeds in pots on her patio off the living room. The patio had glass panels attached to metal rails to protect people and plants from the cool, salty sea breezes and the hungry deer.

She coddled her tomatoes, admiring their voluptuous names like Amana Orange, Black Brandywine, Big Rainbow, deep watering them as the Master Gardener advised, turning their pots toward the sunshine that sifted through the cedar branches of the encircling forest. She picked the lettuce, kale and herbs from her containers for fresh salads, feeling smugly superior to those who bought their produce from the supermarkets in town.

One enterprising young couple took orders by email and left their produce in a cart by the Recycling Centre, where customers picked up their goods on the honour system and left their money in the Free Mail rack, where islanders left messages for one another, in the General Store.

The Professor and his wife were intrigued by how many young people had settled on the island, some of them living on weathered sailboats moored in the harbour.

Another young entrepreneur regularly took the morning ferry to the Big Island where he filled orders for butchered organic chickens from the local farms. He loaded them into his pickup and sold them out of the back of his truck to eager customers who met him down by the dock when he returned on the afternoon ferry.

The local crab fisherman sometimes sold live crab in traps lowered into the water beside his dock. The Professor quickly learned how to pry the hard shells off the crab with the blade of an axe. During the commercial fishing season, a sign on the Wharf Store announced the anticipated arrival of a commercial fishboat from the west coast or northern fishing grounds, loaded with salmon and halibut and prawns for bulk sale to islanders who brought cash and their own containers.

Some islanders set their own crab traps and bought sport fishing licences to fish for salmon and cod, and shared their catch with their neighbours. For those who knew where to look, oysters could still be found on some island beaches.

Posters on the notice board of the General Store warned that Aboriginal hunters with historic rights to the island hunted the local deer in higher forests during the hunting season. They were joined by some old-time islanders, who unlocked their rifles housed in government-licensed cases, and went up the mountain in search of "government game."

But many islanders were squeamish about killing, let alone consuming the tiny white-tailed deer that bounded through their gardens, eating their petunias and young veggies, so tame that they were known to come onto patios in search of potted plants and peer insolently through the windows.

In the early days, Greek hunters from the Mainland arrived on the ferry in their battered trucks, usually before Easter feast days, in search of the young kids of the feral goats that survived on the high meadows of the mountain. The hunters drank their ouzo around their campfire on the fringes of the sheep farm and hunted with the farmer's permission.

Islanders had conflicted views about the goats. Residents who detested the damage the feral goats did to their gardens and pastures advocated for community culls. One frustrated young farmer shocked a community meeting by announcing a mass murder of the scrawny, bearded creatures. "I've killed 150 of the pests," he told his startled audience, "and I am going to kill a lot more."

But when Park biologists supported the community cull of feral goats on the grounds they were not native to the island, the crowd stared them down. "Neither are you guys from Ottawa," someone called out.

The next spring, as soon as the frost left the ground, the Master Gardener taught the Professor's wife how to plant potatoes next to the garlic in her raised box. He dug trenches in the soil, lining them with grass cut from the schoolyard and preparing them for the Yukon Gold seed potatoes she had bought from the garden shop in town. Kneeling down on the soft turf, she carefully placed the potatoes in the trenches.

When she was finished covering them up, she sat back on her heels, breathing in the smell of fresh, fragrant earth, and felt enormously pleased with herself. She pushed herself up onto her feet, turned to her tutor, and asked: "When will they be ready to eat?"

He was proud of his pupil too. "Late August, depending on the summer weather," he told her. "Definitely by Labour Day." He showed her how to plant beans and squash, and how to tuck tiny green peppers and eggplants between the rows.

In late spring, the Master Gardener sent out an email announcing the garlic pull would take place the following Wednesday. It had been delayed by weeks of rain. The Professor's wife parked on the side of the road by the baseball diamond, her containers for her garlic harvest in the trunk of her hatchback. Everyone else was already there, some already imbibing the wine and appies that were part of the harvest ritual.

She placed her wine and cheese puffs on the rough, wooden garden table and looked for a shovel that she had forgotten to bring, not being sure of the garlic pull protocol. The Master Gardener gave her a shovel from several bladed into the earth, like spare soldiers, standing straight and in line. At her garden box, half covered with fierce-looking stalks, she tentatively tipped the toe of the blade into the dirt.

"What happens if I slice the bulb in two?" she asked. No one answered, busy with their own harvest. She dug out a bearded, dirt-caked white bulb of impressive size attached to the fronded stalk. She took the stalk and started shaking it.

"No, no, no!" cried the Master Gardener, grabbing it from her. "Garlic bruises easily. You must be gentle with it." He patted the bulb gently and some dirt fell off. A lot didn't. He laid it on the ground beside the garden box. While the wife dug another head, he told her how to process her harvest. "First, you keep the garlic stalks in the sun, turning them over to dry, and take them in every night for a week."

"Three to five days," corrected the café chef, who had approached her box to see how the newcomer was doing on her initial garlic harvest. "It depends on how sunny it is." He sipped his red wine.

The Master Gardener glared at him. "You leave them in the sun for a week," he repeated. "Then you tie, say, ten bulbs together in a bunch with some string and hang them in a dark place for about three weeks. I use my garage."

"Could I use our generator shack?" the Professor's wife asked. "I only have a carport." She wondered if she had any string, and, for that matter, how she would hang up the garlic bunches.

"Any dark place will do, as long as it is dry," said the fire chief, who had joined the crew encouraging the novice planter. "I tie the bulbs together using the stalks themselves. Hang them for about two weeks."

"Three weeks," the Master Gardener corrected. "And keep them dry." He explained when the beards could be removed from the garlic bulbs and how the bulbs should be cut off, leaving a long stem, "so the juices don't drip out."

The wife was trying to keep up. "So first I hang the bulbs up for a week and then I dry them out in the sun for three weeks, turning them over . . ."

"No, no, no," interrupted the Master Gardener. "You have it backwards. Dry in the sun first, then hang in the dark." He went off to inspect the harvests of the other garlic gardeners.

The wife carefully dug up the rest of the bulbs that glowed like white skulls through their earth-encrusted beards. She patted each one free of dirt and laid them gently on the ground and counted twenty-three garlic heads. She stepped back to admire her harvest, breathing deeply, proudly, and shook the dirt from her gloves.

She joined the others at the garden bar. They were pouring wine into plastic glasses and eating crackers and pesto made from the young garlic scapes, overtly examining each grower's harvest to compare numbers and sizes. The café chef described his recipe for his dip. "Cut up a garlic head, add jalapeno pepper, pour soy sauce over mixture, and let it bubble in the fridge for six months," he explained.

She spread some dip on a cracker and tasted it. Hot, but

delicious. Buster the Garden Dog, a regular winner at the Pet Show's Best Tricks event, showed off—sitting up, bowing down, rolling over in the dirt, barking, turning in circles. He ran off to torment the feral cats stalking around the Cat House, barking loudly at the latest arrival, a black and grey striped male, who hissed back at him, pawing the fence with its claws.

Sipping the wine from their plastic cups, the gardeners discussed how the birds knew when fruit was ready to harvest—it was their vision powers, they decided—and how the raccoons robbed the apple trees the night before a planned pick.

The boxes in the community garden looked denuded without the garlic stalks, although some boxes still housed green beans and squash and some yellow-flowered tomato plants. The wife checked her own plants and wondered how anything had grown in the squishy soil, given all the rain.

One lone box stood untouched and unharvested. It was known that the couple who rented it was having marital problems. Responsibility for the garlic pull or even ownership of the prized bulbs might be an issue.

When the wine and appies had been consumed, the garlic gardeners, regretful that the season was over, gathered up their gloves and shovels and returned to their homes. The Professor's wife looked at the garlic harvest in the trunk of the car and wondered what to do with it. When she arrived home she found a canvas wheelbarrow and transferred the crop into it and left the barrow in the garage.

The next morning when she returned to the carport, her dilemma unresolved, she found one garlic stalk had been pulled out of the wheelbarrow and left on the concrete floor. "I must ask the Master Gardener whether raccoons eat garlic," she told the Professor, whose only interest in his wife's garlic harvest was in the eating of it. She wheeled the barrow over to the woodpile and distributed the garlic stalks over the tarp covering so that they caught the sun.

An hour later, she realized that the sun had shifted. The garlic was now in shadow, so she loaded the garlic onto a garbage bag and carried it though the living room and spread it on the stone patio in the front of the house. I must remember to take it in at night, she reminded herself.

She picked up a bearded bulb of garlic, brushed away the shards of soil and lifted it to her nose, inhaling its sharp, bittersweet aroma, hinting of future stews, steaks on the barbeque, maybe even garlic jam. I may not have a green thumb, she thought, but I will settle for a garlic one!

BLONDIE

THE PROFESSOR'S WIFE FIRST SAW them at the island pet show, the beautiful blonde with her golden retriever, both blessed with long, flowing honey tresses and great legs. They won the Best Look-Alike award, defeating the perennial winners, the white highland terrier and his white-haired owner, who pulled her hair into a white terrier-like tuft. The audience cheered from their canvas chairs on the sidelines of the island ballpark.

She was known as Blondie. The retriever was called Goldie.

She saw them again at the Saturday Recycling Centre, and they became tentative friends as they searched for abandoned garden tools, hoses, and jam and pickle jars, piled on shelves that festooned the Free Store at the Recycling Centre. When Blondie delightedly pulled a window frame with glass intact from a pile of lumber, the wife asked, "Are you going to use that for a cold frame?"

"No," said Blondie, scrounging through the construction litter in the Recycling shed. "I need it for the house I'm building up the mountain." She lugged the window frame, along with her other treasures, to the ancient Jeep parked outside Recycling's chain fence. Over cups of decaf coffee in the café, the wife gently prodded the musician to tell her more.

Blondie and her partner, survivors of the back-to-the-land hippie era, came to the island from a commune up the coast and acquired an isolated fragment of land on the mountain bordering the sheep farm below. They lived in a tent mounted on a wooden floor. For the first few years, every time Blondie complained of the cold, damp accommodation, her partner threw another plastic cover over the tent and resumed his task of restoring an old car he had pulled out of a ditch in the valley.

Finally fed up, Blondie found a spool of carpenter string, chopped some stakes from the cedar wood pile, and borrowed a book from the library called *Build Your Own House: A How-To Guide for Beginners*. A trained musician who had played in the Symphony in town in her former life, she had never held a hammer in her hands, although her dirt-encrusted fingernails were testimony to her hard work grubbing in her veggie garden.

Her nose in the book, Blondie paced off the dimensions of her cabin, pounded in her stakes, and strung her carpenter string to mark the exterior walls. She found out years later that the property line ran through her kitchen. She used recycled lumber to build the forms for her concrete footings.

When he realized she was serious, her partner remounted the engine in the old car, replaced the flat tires with newer ones from another wreck, and drove off island.

And when the islanders became aware of what she was doing, a curious migration took place up the mountain. Local tradesmen and carpenters, their normal shifts finished, appeared on the cabin site with equipment and advice and, most importantly, their helping hands, although Blondie worked along with the best of them, learning and observing.

Walls went up. Windows were wrestled into place, not an easy task because the lumber cut in the local mill from local timber was not the dimension grade found in the lumber stores. An island two-by-four measured two by four, not the more refined 1¾ by 3¾ produced in the larger mills on the Big Island.

A staircase, which is always tricky to build and beyond Blondie's skills, was installed into the space behind the field-stone fireplace, the work of the island's much-sought-after stonemason, who curiously had the time to work on the site while frustrated paying customers in their waterfront homes left messages on his answering machine.

An accomplished furniture maker showed up with a front door crafted from yellow cedar. When she saw it, the Professor's wife bit her lip with envy. She and her husband couldn't afford a yellow cedar door for their modest waterfront cottage.

The only person who never made it up the abandoned logging trail to the top was the building inspector responsible for the island, although if he craned his neck when he was riding in his truck and looked up he could see the small structure perched high above the cliffs where the eagles gyrated in the warm thermals. But why would he bother to look up?

"I have enough work to do on island without risking my tires driving God knows where and finding God knows what and to no good purpose," he grumbled over a beer in the pub. He added that islanders were living in worse places, rehabilitated chicken houses and dilapidated barns, and in one case a converted container parked among the cedars.

Slowly the house on the hilltop took shape. Solar panels were mounted on the roof and a hand shower recycled from a sailboat was attached to a wall on the side porch where only the goats could view a blonde bathing in the buff. A wood stove with a hot water reservoir was hauled up the trail and installed in the small kitchen where the musician made tea and cookies for her workforce.

Slowly the island tradesmen finished their tasks and packed up their tools and drove down the hill. Blondie hung her curtains, moved her things from the tent she had shared with her former partner, and settled in. Her own house. Built with her own hands. And with a little help from her friends.

At first, she was content. Over the wind-warmed, sun-kissed summer she planted her herb garden and stacked the wood for winter. She sat on her porch, playing her guitar and composing new songs. The view of distant islands moored in the sea below was her muse.

She saw the orcas swim by, could hear their snorts and squeals. She monitored the movement of deep-sea ships bound for the Big City. Her dog, Goldie, played with a golden kitty and chased the feral goats that pastured on the hillside.

When she found an ancient spinet piano at Recycling, Blondie had it hauled up the hill in the back of the baker's truck.

"How are you going to have it tuned all the way up here?" asked the Professor's wife as she admired the piano's golden woodwork and yellowed keys.

"I haven't crossed that bridge yet," admitted Blondie, sorting through her piano music and positioning family photos on top of the instrument.

She did when a famous pianist touring the islands on a Canada Council grant, accompanied by his white concert grand and a piano tuner, gave a performance in the Community Hall. Blondie billeted the piano tuner at her cabin up the hill, who obligingly tuned her spinet in exchange for her oven-baked biscuits and blueberry tea.

Visitors streamed up the hill to the cabin bearing wine and home-grown veggies, luscious plums and tart apples from island orchards, pies and casseroles for sunset suppers. Blondie enjoyed her solitude and never minded when they returned to their own homes, supplied with hydro power and laptop computers and television programs. She drove down to the General Store for mail and supplies and occasionally a concert or lecture in the Community Hall.

In late summer she invited her island girlfriends up for dinner. "A girls' night out," she said, and included the newcomer, the Professor's wife, in her guest list. Her guests arrived in a small convoy of cars, doubling up to save gas and the environment, bringing wine, fish, chutney and brownies, and gales of laughter.

Outside the cabin windows a rain front advanced from the southwest, canvasses of clouds trailing tails of rain showers behind them. Behind the rain, sunlight dappled the sea below where a red-hulled freighter moved slowly through the Strait.

After dinner, Blondie took the women outside to watch her feed her family of feral goats. In the surreal light of dusk, the herd came up the hill over the cropped alpine meadow grass to feed on hay piled beyond the fenced garden. Goldie chased away a small black billy goat, and Blondie's little golden cat ran in circles between their hairy legs, advancing and then darting away.

Her feral family included one white goat and a small black goat with a white belt on one flank and a white spot on the other. The goats stared at the guests, gathered with their wine glasses on the patio, sunset glinting off the cabin windows. They stared back at the goats and at Blondie, slim and lovely in her tight-fitting jeans, long-sleeved top, and her long blond hair, feeding the goats grapevines from her hand.

A pagan princess-of-the-harvest, the Professor's wife thought, absorbing the beauty of the moment. Lightning slashed through the dark sky on the drive home, and rain spattered on the windshield. Autumn's outriders.

Blondie, navigating her Jeep down the muddy trail that at times was more like a mountain streamlet, didn't mind the endless downpour of the autumn rains.

But then came winter. Heavy, wet snow blocked the trail. Then 100-kilometre-an-hour winds whiplashed the trees, bending them to the rocky ground, confining her and Goldie to the cabin. When the wind died in the gloom of a winter dawn, she pulled on her snow boots, put on her Free Store parka and gloves, picked up her chainsaw, let herself and Goldie out the door, and surveyed the damage wrought by the storm.

The snow was deep, hunched up against the cabin and the shed, burying the hubcaps of her Jeep. Tree branches broken off by the gusts were carelessly tossed about on the snow. The old logging road down to the valley was blocked with trees felled by the storm. She sighed, picked up her chainsaw, clumped through the drifts to the first downed tree, started up the chainsaw, and commenced bucking the wood into stove lengths.

Hours later, as the white sun overhead signaled noon, she was almost halfway down the hill when she met three of her neighbours on the logging road. She had heard the sound of their chainsaws earlier, whining through the still air as they started from the bottom of the logging road where the snowplow had stopped, and began clearing the broken trees that barred her path.

They were worried about her, they explained, wiping the sweat from their faces with their work mitts. She could have slipped into a tree well and suffocated in the snow. She could have sliced her leg with her chainsaw. They offered all manner of doomsday possibilities before picking up the chainsaws and completing their work so that when the snow melted she could drive her Jeep out. They pulled a bag of groceries out of a backpack.

Nice neighbours, she thought, offering them her water bottle.

That winter, Blondie came down with a bad case of flu. For the first time she became afraid of her isolation in the cold, creaking cabin. She shivered beneath her blanket as her wood box emptied; the woodpile was stacked under the trees outside beyond her reach. Her cell phone didn't work. She realized she could fall into a coma, even die, and nobody would know what had happened to her. If she couldn't drive down, neighbours couldn't drive up to check on her.

When the winds died down and the snow thawed, and she felt she might survive after all, Blondie drove down the hill and onto the ferry and headed for the nearest Canadian Tire store. There she selected a telephone and a large spool of telephone extension cord and wheeled it to the checkout counter.

"What are you planning to do with all that cord?" asked the clerk skeptically.

"You don't want to know," replied Blondie. "But I need at least a kilometre for what I have in mind."

The clerk shook his head and helped her load the spool onto a cart.

When Blondie arrived home, she plugged one end of the extension cord into her telephone base and threaded it through the wall of her kitchen. Outside the cabin she strung the extension cord over the ground, clearing away the wet branches and rocks sticking through decaying snow-drifts, down the hill to a box on the telephone pole beside the road below. To her great relief she had enough cord for her purpose. Blondie was now connected to the world.

As time went by she met a new partner, a skilled carpenter who built an addition to the cabin. Eventually they installed a satellite internet connection. Her partner borrowed a road grader and smoothed the trail.

But the over-the-ground extension cord, exposed to the elements and the random hoofs of the feral goats and deer and by curious dogs in search of voles and rodents, survived, although at times the connection was faint, as if the telephone call was coming from another planet.

Maybe it is, the wife thought as she finished her conversation with Blondie about an upcoming concert and hung up the phone. Maybe one day it will.

BATS IN THE BELFRY

THE REDHEADED WOMAN PRIEST WAS working on the island's public dock with the Mountie from the local RCMP detachment, cleaning and hosing down the Canadian Coast Guard Auxiliary's Zodiac after a joint training session on the Salish Sea with the police and Coast Guard volunteers.

When she was assigned to her island parish, the priest joined the CCG Auxiliary, rescuing vacationing landlubbers who ran out of gas, towing tide-stranded boats off the rocks, and pulling people out of the freezing ocean. Her house was only minutes from the wharf where the rescue boat was docked, as required of all maritime rescue volunteers.

"I have a problem," she said, hosing the cleaning detergent off her rubber boots before turning the hose on the rescue boat. "There are bats in the church."

The Mountie stopped scrubbing the interior of the boat. "What are you talking about?" he asked his companion, who looked like a sea witch with her red curls tangled by the wind, in her foul-weather jacket, pants, and boots.

"Bats," she said. She certainly had his attention. "They are living in the church arches under the roof. They shit on the pews and their urine stains the Communion chalices. And they stink."

"What are you going to do?" asked the Mountie. He was fond of his crew mate, although he kept his feelings hidden, whatever that means on an island where everybody knew everything about everyone else.

"I am going to close the church until the bats leave in the fall," she replied, turning off the water tap on the dock and coiling the hose into its box at the bottom of the gangway.

The Mountie sighed. His detachment covered several islands in the Salish Sea. His problems were routine: people smuggling ciggies into Canada from the American islands across the International Boundary waters, others smuggling pot back across the strait, speeders on the narrow island roads.

The last breaking and entering case he dealt with involved a man who was spotted disappearing into the bushes of the community park on the neighbour island with an outboard motor mounted on his backpack. Islanders tackled the thief, tied him up to a picnic table, and supplied him with cigarettes and sandwiches until the police boat arrived.

He knew his friend was facing a challenge. She had three strikes against her. First, she was a woman priest. Second, she was an off-islander. And third, she introduced changes in the Anglican service that unsettled some members of her small congregation, scattered across three churches on three islands.

She replaced the four-hundred-year-old Book of Common Prayer with the newfangled Book of Alternative Services, adopted in the 20th century. She abandoned the King James version of the Bible for a newer edition, with more modern language. Simple words for simpletons, thought the Church Warden, although he did not say that to her face.

She introduced non-traditional Taizé services that focused on singing and chanting. She wheedled and whined until the lady members of the Altar Guild agreed to replace the carpets. These changes were not universally popular among members of her congregation, particularly the older ones, although the scattering of younger ones liked the guitar music.

The Rector, as she preferred to be called, was a break with tradition herself. New to the parish, female, and a transplanted Nova Scotian, the redhead lived on a neighbouring island. She met her south island congregation for the first time at her introductory Parish Potluck held at the home of the Church Warden and his wife.

It is axiomatic that twice as many people show up for the Parish Potlucks than those who actually attend church, drawn by good food and good company and the opportunity for titillating gossip. On that score the new Rector delivered.

The group comprised a retired sheep farmer and his

wife, the Sunday school teacher, and other pillars of the community, including the sour-faced church treasurer and the local self-proclaimed heretic who came for the free food. After they had collected their plates of baked salmon, crab dip, and bean salad and settled into their seats, the Church Warden turned to the Rector and said genially, "Now there, why don't you tell us about yourself."

"Well, I grew up in Nova Scotia, took a teaching degree at Dalhousie University, and married a classmate who studied law," the Rector began, sitting up straight in her reclining chair and placing her plate on her knees. The members of the congregation nodded approvingly.

"Then I found out he was an alcoholic, so I divorced him," the Rector continued. She sipped her wild blueberry herb tea made from berries collected and dried by two struggling young organic farmers on the island.

Some members of the congregation clucked uncertainly. Despite Charles and Diana and other members of the Royal Family, divorce still seemed, well, un-Anglican. The old sheep farmer jolted forward on his chair, his palsied hand spilling his coffee. His wife patted his knee soothingly.

"Afterward, I felt the call to the church, so I went to seminary to study theology," she continued, ignoring the clicks of disapproval. "There I met my second husband, an Anglican theologian and a professor at the seminary where I was his student," the Rector continued. "We received special permission from the Church to marry."

The church treasurer's eyes bulged and the salmon on his fork paused on the journey to his mouth. The local heretic enjoyed the moment and the bean salad. This was better than a reality television show.

The Church Warden was uncharacteristically at a loss for words. To end the silence that followed the Rector's announcement, he asked what they all wanted to know. "What brought you to our island parish?"

"When my husband passed on, I read your parish advertisement in the *Anglican Journal* and asked the Bishop for a transfer," she answered, sipping her tea and pushing away an arrogant tabby cat who was trying to swipe a piece of salmon from her plate.

A widow, then. Somewhat mollified, the members of the congregation rose from their chairs and headed to the table for more coffee, tea, and brownies before returning home. Everyone knows what Maritimers are like. All those dreary novels about incest and adultery and dysfunctional families that win the CanLit book prizes and top the bestseller lists.

In fact, the Rector had applied for the three-island, three-church parish because she loved the sea. On her arrival she persuaded the parish council to buy a church boat for inter-island travel. A parishioner obligingly provided one, a twenty-one-foot Bayliner in which the Rector, in all kinds of weather, zoomed about the channels separating the islands.

She valued her role as a fisher of men, both on- and offshore. "It is very rewarding to be involved in saving someone's life," she confided to the Mountie over coffee in her rustic kitchen, where ceramic cats napped on the well-scrubbed counters. She had made him a batch of his favourite sugar cookies.

They met when she and her crew returned a stolen boat to the dock and filed a report at the police station. The Mountie was assigned to the detachment to replace a woman RCMP constable who was afraid of boats, a handicap in a policing area that covered the islands in the Salish Sea.

"There is nothing more beautiful than the sun rising over the ocean when we have been out all night on a search, and the sky lightens and then turns crimson-streaked with gold and pink, and the water reflects the colours," the Rector continued. Her friend was silent as he sipped his coffee and reached for a cookie. He found nothing romantic about nighttime police or rescue missions.

She described a night patrol when the phosphorescence in the water turned the boat's wake into a river of liquid silver. "When I looked over the side of the boat it was as though a million bits of confetti were slowly rising and falling through the water, and the salmon were silver streaks approaching and then curving away from the boat," she said, pushing away a live cat that was investigating the plate of sugar cookies on her kitchen table.

"One night, a silver fountain bubbled through the sea as a seal came up for air while Orion wheeled through the night sky," she told him. Those nights on the water were Holy. She didn't see how anyone could experience that and not believe in a Creator. Smiling, feeling somehow cheered, the Mountie finished his coffee and left to resume his normal rounds.

Island life followed its seasonal tides. Autumn faded into winter. Spring blossomed into summer.

Parish life continued peacefully, despite the grumblings of some parishioners who disliked female priests on principle. There were pancake breakfasts and parish picnics, weddings and funerals, flower shows and garden parties, and occasional movie nights on selected topics with environmental themes. Environmentalist David Suzuki's taped television shows were particularly popular.

Then the bats invaded the church.

They arrived in the spring, roused from their long winter sleep, their genetic clock ticking with the need to breed. A number selected the church arches for their maternity roosts, spending their summer days hanging upside down from the rafters, or flying from one roost to another, the pups clinging to their mother's undersides.

When they became aware of the intruders, members of the congregation who cared about the environment debated whether they were of the big brown bat or the little brown bat myotis species. Others mentioned nervously that humans can contract rabies from bats and die a horrible death. No one in the congregation found them cute.

The redheaded Rector found them repulsive. One Sunday she pointed to the bat droppings on the pews and the urine-stained chalices. The Church Warden's wife shuddered and the organist examined the keys of her instrument for signs of bat excrement.

But no one knew what to do. Bats were protected under the Wildlife Act and could not be indiscriminately killed. The Church Warden opened all the windows of the church and turned off the lights, hoping the bats would leave on their own. The Rector sent for the Environment Department's Safe and Sensible Pest Control pamphlet on bats, which had little to say about bats already in residence.

But the bats hung in there.

Finally, the Rector found an answer to her prayers. She announced the church must be closed until the bats left in the fall, when foam insulation could be sprayed to block the holes under the eaves to prevent them from returning in the spring. Until then, she declared, church services would be held in the Community Hall down by the ferry wharf.

The church treasurer objected. "We've always had bats in church," he told the woman priest. A retired accountant, he carefully managed the church's fragile finances. He disliked the changes introduced by the Rector and ignored her Words and Music offerings, declaring them not real church services. He rarely attended the visiting American minister's interdenominational services, and he thought meditation in the church should be banned. Well, at least restricted to real Buddhists.

He refused to attend the Community Hall services.

Sitting outside in his car, he sent his wife in to pick up the collection and contributions to the Development Fund. He had nothing against the Community Hall, where church services had been held before the upside-down-boat church was built, but renting the Hall was not in the budget.

Secretly, in his heart of hearts, he had never accepted the decision to allow women priests in the Anglican Church. What is the world coming to? he mused, as he counted the bills and coins in the collection plate, entering the total on the proper forms. They will be blessing homosexuals next.

He refused to authorize the purchase of a new copy machine, forcing the Rector to crank out each Sunday's Order of Service pamphlet on the old hand-operated machine. He complained when she asked the service man to check the fuel tank for the emergency generator when it leaked fuel and fumes into the Fair Trade shop in the church basement, which remained open for business.

The Church Warden and other church members faithfully attended the Community Hall services, but they were powerless in the face of the truculent treasurer's reluctance to support the Rector's efforts to resume services in the church itself only when the bat invasion was resolved. Secretly, some of them preferred the informality of the Hall that was less, well, religious. More like group therapy with hymns.

When the bats finally left in the fall to forage for their winter food and no one took steps to prevent their return to the little church, the redheaded Rector, her prayers for patience unanswered, removed her priestly stole with its embroidered golden cross and packed her bags. She told the Mountie, "I can't deal with this any longer. I quit."

"It's no sin to stop putting up with bat shit," the Mountie consoled her.

She turned in her keys to the parish Bayliner and bought her own boat. She applied to the Bishop for an appointment to a church on a northern island and joined the local Coast Guard Auxiliary. The Mountie applied for a transfer to her new parish and they were married there by another woman priest the following spring.

In the resulting scramble to clean up the bat droppings on the church pews and floors and scrub the Communion chalices and find a replacement Rector in a priest-poor parish, no one thought to block the bat entry holes under the attic eaves during the winter months.

The Bishop sent a new priest to serve the island parish. The new priest was a rumpled sort of man, with a vague manner and a vacant look. His sentences trailed off into unfinished questions. He talked about Emotional Intelligence and Affirmative Thinking and other concepts not normally discussed over post-Communion coffee in the church basement.

Still the congregation was prepared to cut him some slack. They prided themselves on being open minded. They read Karen Armstrong's *Twelve Steps to a Compassionate World* at the book club, and reminded one another of the

Golden Rule: do unto others as you would like them to do unto you. Or most of the time.

The Church Warden's wife, however, sat through the services in a state of anxiety. The new priest couldn't seem to deliver a recognizable Anglican service. Was he going to conduct the services in his shirt sleeves (horrors!) or would he wear his clerical stole?

He rarely had a printed Order of Service like the United Church minister did, setting out the hymns and the prayers. He selected hymns from three different hymn books, causing some confusion as the congregation tried to find the right hymn in the right book while the organist gamely played on.

He chose the Apostle's Creed because, he told the congregation thumbing through the prayer book, "it is short." Sometimes he said that they didn't have to say it at all because the people on the neighbour island had recited it earlier that Sunday. He forgot to include the General Confession—the Church Warden's wife enjoyed recounting her modest sins—and the General Thanksgiving that allowed her to reflect on the equally modest blessings of her life.

Her state of nerves peaked when he decided to ask the congregation to form a circle and serve each other the wine in the silver Communion cup and the wafer on its silver plate instead of serving it himself to people kneeling at the Communion rail, as traditional churches did, even the United Church minister, who explained that since her church was set up during the Temperance Movement, the Communion cup contained only grape juice.

The problem was nobody could recall the correct responses as they served each other the wine and the wafers.

Worse, the Absent-Minded Priest, as she referred to him privately, usually forgot to call for the collection plate to be passed around, which infuriated the Church Warden who was responsible for the little church's precarious existence. "God does not pay the Hydro bill," he fumed, pacing in his study after they returned from church services.

Somehow they managed to maintain the church over the winter. No one told the new priest about a potential bat invasion.

The next spring, the bats came back.

PET PARADE

THE OFF-ISLANDER'S SECRET AMBITION WAS to win a prize in the island's Pet Parade, where the island dogs displayed their owners in a ritual as predictable as the autumn equinox. The off-islander lived in town with his wife and children, his English setter, Rupert, and the calico cat, commuting regularly to their weekend cottage on island to conduct business and enjoy island life.

He earned his living selling island real estate, sometimes feeling like a vulture, circling the carrion of failed marriages and funerals and the fate of older islanders who were carted off island in Dora, the ancient ambulance, to chronic care wards in town, never to return.

The people who lived on island and off island had their issues. When he first came to the island, the realtor shared a telephone line with a local fisherman. Sometimes, when the off-islander was on the phone, his call would be interrupted by the fisherman who complained, "You are a weekender. You're only supposed to use the phone on weekends. We locals get to use the phone on weekdays."

Usually the off-islander obligingly hung up, clearing the phone line for the fisherman.

He joined the island's Men's Club and the service club, which was pretty well mandatory, and played bridge with the elders in the Community Hall on Friday afternoons when he was on island, but even after fifteen years as a part-time resident he still felt self-conscious in his fleece and faded jeans.

Winning an event at the Pet Parade, calculated the off-islander, would gain him acceptance among the island residents. Maybe Rupert could win him the respect he longed for.

The pet show was presented in the ballpark situated in the valley, sponsored by the island's service club. Admission was free. Dogs and their owners paid ten dollars to register.

The audience sat in metal chairs under white canopies borrowed from the Community Hall, studying their programs with the intensity of racetrack regulars studying their racing forms. Their restless children played in the outfield, ringed with golden gorse blazing against the green cedars.

A wet wind from the sea was rising in bursts that threatened to bring the canopies down on the crowd. Some people clung to the metal posts that supported the canvas to shelter themselves from the impending rain.

Along with the more traditional events, such as Best Trick and Best Retriever, were less challenging categories, such as Shake a Paw, or Whitest Teeth, or Happiest/Saddest Dog. The off-islander wistfully hoped Rupert would win People's Choice Best of the Winners. He did not want his candidate to claim the Haven't Won a Prize All Day award.

The judges for the Pet Parade sat at their own table at the side of the grassy patch where the event was staged. They included the wharf manager, who attached cotton floppy dog ears to his own and dressed in the costume of the Hanging Judge who executed justice in the BC Interior during the nineteenth-century gold rush.

The others included the island baker, known as the Green Giant for his impassioned commitment to environmental issues, the island's much-loved oldest resident with her blue eyes and English rose complexion, and the local fire chief who was doing double duty as a volunteer, since the 1967 fire engine was parked beside the barbeque pit that advertised a variety of "dogs"—veggie dogs, jumbo all-beef dogs, cheddar smokies—as well as soda pop and water.

Next to the judges was a table loaded with the coveted prizes, neon-coloured toy animals collected from flea markets and garage sales on the the Mainland and donated by a spike-haired artist who dressed in a rainbow collection of various wraps, skirts, and hoodies selected from the Free Store at the Recycling Centre, the only fashion outlet on the island with the exception of the Avon Lady.

The off-islander sat on his metal chair in the front row with the other nervous contenders. The wind stirred the canopy fringe overhead. His wife sat beside him nursing her coffee in her recycled coffee mug. She owned a hair salon in town. Her bleached blond pageboy was streaked with brown and red tints, reminiscent of Burberry plaid. Her rotund buttocks encased in her too-tight jeans made her a likely candidate for the Cutest Booty (Dog and/or Owner) prize. Their setter Rupert panted at their feet.

The genial Master of Ceremonies, an organic gardener in his workday world, picked up the mic from the judges' table and called all contestants and their owners onto the field for the traditional walkabout and Best Dressed Dog event. The MC's usual good humour had been tested by demands from the Park Warden that all dogs were to be leashed, since the ballpark was technically in the National Park. Various permits were required, according to the rules set out in distant Ottawa.

Two of the dogs on parade stopped, squatted, and did their business on the grass in front of the watchful Park Warden. The crowd under the canopies tittered approvingly.

Eleven dogs paraded their owners around for the Best Dressed Dog competition. All the dogs were more stylishly dressed than their owners, who wore T-shirts and jeans and Cowichan sweaters. The two golden retrievers sported tartan blankets on their backs and tam o'shanters on their heads.

The pug wore a chic tan jacket, fastened under her belly with fashionable gold buttons.

The off-islander dragged a reluctant Rupert onto the field. The setter wore a coat styled along the lines of a smoking jacket that fit his English remittance-man image. The wife with the plaid hair yelled, "Go, Rupert, go!" Which he did, peeing in front of the judges' table.

The tartan-clothed retrievers won first prize, which was fair, because the audience knew that they were banned from more difficult events like Best Retrievers, on the grounds they were too well trained. The pug won second prize. Rupert won Honorable Mention, to the relief of the off-islander. He made his way to the judges' table to select a stuffed, shocking pink poodle. At least there wouldn't be a Haven't Won a Prize All Day in Rupert's future.

There followed in quick succession the Most Glamorous and Most Handsome awards and the Dog and Dog Owner Look-alike, won as usual by the pretty white-haired islander who shamelessly styled her hair to match her shaggy white westie, tying matching ribbons on both their hairdos.

Rupert did not win or place in either event.

He did better in the tail-wagging competition, swinging his elegantly feathered tail in front of the judges' faces to place third to the black and blond cocker spaniels, with their gyrating hips and cheerleader tails, and beating out Reggie, the beagle mix with the short legs and low-slung belly.

It was clear to the off-islander that Reggie was the dog to

beat for the Best of the Winners award. A crowd favourite and winner of the Best Vocal event, Reggie could be counted on to be a serious contender for Best Trick or the Obstacle Race that was, in fact, designed by Reggie's owner.

The judges sat at their table, studying their forms and rating the contenders in an arbitrary manner, based on best performance coupled with personal preferences. Their work was complicated by the lobbying of the oldest resident on behalf on an aged collie named Lucy with a shaggy coat and no perceptible talent beyond that of getting in everybody's way.

When the other judges pointed out that Lucy dropped the ball, or never completed the course, or in one case actually left the field altogether, the oldest resident persisted, "But she tries so hard. Don't you think she rates at least an Honourable Mention?"

The other judges sighed and shrugged their shoulders. Honorable Mention it was.

While the judges conferred, the crowd stood, stretched, and collected coffee and hot dogs from the busy barbeque volunteers before returning to their canopies. Now for the more difficult events.

First was Best Behaved Dog. The off-islander had spent weeks training Rupert in the discipline of come, sit, stay, but Rupert never got the hang of it, standing when he should sit, sitting when he should come. He did better in the Worst Behaved category, coming in first. The off-islander and his wife were ecstatic. The children were thrilled. Worst Behaviour was cool.

Next was Best Retriever. Chester, a golden Labrador, found the thrown ball in the outfield but was disqualified when he made a long detour around the entire ball field, to the cheers of the crowd, before returning the ball to his sheepish owner. Reggie was on the ball like a shot and returned it to his owner's feet, wagging his short tail happily.

Rupert watched his owner throw the ball in an easy, underhand motion. The off-islander had high hopes for Rupert, whose most annoying parlour trick was retrieving the butter dish from a neighbour's picnic table. But instead the setter sat down, signaling in his best "I say, old boy, not today" manner that he was not up to the challenge. "He has never done that before," said the humiliated off-islander.

Reggie won.

The program was interrupted when a sudden gust of wind tipped over one of the white canopies, shrouding the startled audience seated below. After people emerged from the folds of canvas and wrestled the canopy upright, securing it in place, they resumed their seats and the pet performance continued.

The highlight of the day was the Obstacle Race. This consisted of a series of hoops, ladders, chairs, and finally a slide positioned in the middle of the grassy show ring. The owners walked their dogs on the sidelines, furtively feeding their pets to maintain the canine contestants' interest.

Chester completed the race to cheers, placing a paw on each ladder rung and jumping up on the chairs, but balking at the slide. The judges pondered how to weigh the results of completing some obstacles but not all of them.

The collie Lucy jumped off the ladder at the midway point, ignored the chairs, and ran around the hoops instead of through them. "Definitely worth an Honorable Mention," the oldest resident said loyally.

Reggie's owner, spilling tidbits from her pockets, ran through the hoops herself. Reggie followed her. She coaxed him along the ladder, up onto the chairs and, after some false starts, down the slide and into the winner's circle.

Reggie won again.

After the Parade of Champions, Reggie was acclaimed People's Choice Best of the Winners, as usual. He took home the biggest stuffed dog of all. Chester won the Haven't Won a Prize All Day award and a dog dish. The judge with the floppy cotton dog ears attached to his own won People's Choice Best Judge.

The off-islander picked up Rupert's leash, his prized ribbons lettered in gold, his stuffed toy prizes, and his wife, who did win the Cutest Booty (Dog and /or Owner) award.

He was happy with their winnings. And there was always next year.

BATTLE FOR THE BEACH

THE POSTER ON THE FREE MAIL bulletin board, hung near the post office in the General Store, blared in black letters:

CRIME ALERT
RECENTLY SEVERAL BEACH ACCESS
SIGNS IDENTIFYING PUBLIC ACCESS ROUTES
HAVE BEEN STOLEN AND VANDALIZED
POLICE HAVE BEEN NOTIFIED
IF YOU HAVE ANY INFORMATION
ON THE PERSONS RESPONSIBLE
PLEASE CALL THE RCMP
YOU ARE GUARANTEED ANONYMITY
REWARD WILL BE PAID

The Church Warden's wife read the poster as she stood in line to get the mail at the post office in the General Store. She shivered. Always an anxious person, visions of vandals in the night slashing signposts unnerved her. It was such a peaceful island.

And it would upset the Church Warden. Never good news. More harrumphing. Letters to the editor. Flyers sent to island residents stuffed in the Free Mail rack.

"What is this all about?" asked the Professor's wife, coming up behind her in the lineup, clutching her freshly stamped letters. The two women had met on Beach Cleanup Day and were becoming tentative friends, the long-time resident mentoring the new arrival on the intricacies of island life.

"It is a long-running war," replied the Church Warden's wife. "The battle for the beaches. The right of people to have access to public beaches, or the waterfront below the high tide mark. Some property owners don't want the riff-raff on the beach below their waterfront homes and chase them off."

She did not add that many of the opposing owners were foreigners, usually Americans, often new arrivals, unaware that in Canada public access to most waterfront is an ancient right, probably reflecting a person's need to access the sea and his boat from his home in the days when fishing for food and travel by boat were essential to survival. The Queen's beaches were also protected in many Aboriginal claims.

"We thought we had won the fight here on island," she added. "After all, the beaches belong to the Crown. And public access to them through public right-of-ways is the law. But it looks like we were wrong. Someone is continuing the battle." She dug her own letters out of her string bag to check that she had stamped them. Sometimes she forgot and they were returned, handed back to her discreetly by the Postmistress.

The regular Postmistress was on medical leave. She was so adept at her work that she spent her time knitting multicoloured sweaters and reading pocket books from the Five-Cent Lending Library located on the stationary shelves in the General Store. Her substitute was not so swift, puzzling over the computer equipment, searching for parcels, and looking up postal codes.

As the lineup stalled, the two women decided to have coffee in the store café and settled at the long table where the off-island insurance agents and accountants met with their on-island clients to conduct their business. The Church Warden's wife poured milk and spooned three teaspoons of sugar into her Fair Trade coffee—the newcomer drank her coffee black—and recounted the battle for the beach.

"Once upon a time—actually, fairly recently—the Island Parks Committee decided to position a small bench on a public right-of-way over on the Gulf side overlooking the public beach," she said. "That way the old and the infirm and the just plain tired could enjoy the view of the ocean, the islands, the sunrise, and the snow-covered mountains of the Mainland."

The newcomer clutched her coffee cup and nodded knowingly. She had heard some of this before from the real estate agent when she and her husband were looking for property to buy.

"The site is grass-covered, flat, and beside a public road, so people would have no trouble accessing the bench. Not everybody can scramble down that bank or walk on the shale rocks—you know how slimy they can be, covered with seaweed when the tide goes out—or walk on the pebbled beaches," continued the Church Warden's wife, warming to her story. She was enjoying this, getting into the rhythm of it. Her husband rarely listened to her island stories, preferring to stretch out in his recliner, watching television, his tabby cat curled on his lap.

"Most of the property owners nearby welcomed the bench. The family who lives next door regularly mows the grass of the public access to reduce the fire hazard. But one couple did not. They launched a counteroffensive.

"They chased people off the beach, telling them it was private property and warning them of the presence of dangerous rattlesnakes—ah, the dreaded Pacific rattler—and poisonous jellyfish and the threat of police arrest.

"The jellyfish are harmless. There are no rattlesnakes—or police—on island. But when beach-walkers persisted, the couple barricaded the bench property lines with yellow police tape marked DANGER in black ink.

"They circulated petitions warning that criminals would arrive by boat in the night and carry out home invasions, tying up terrified homeowners with duct tape and stealing their valuables. Some off-island property owners believed them.

"Signatures were collected. Petitions were signed. Speeches were made. Letters were written to authorities. The bench project was placed on hold by bureaucrats on the Big Island, who hardly ever come here to check things out."

The newcomer again nodded her head. She was aware of the tension that sometimes existed between the off-island property owners who rarely visited their waterfront lots and held them mainly as investments or for their retirement at some far-off future date, showing little interest in island affairs unless their own rights were affected.

"Many islanders were angry at the attempt by the private owners to hijack public beaches," recounted the Church Warden's wife. She stood up and pushed back her chair, reaching for the coffee carafe to refill their coffee cups, keeping an eye on the post office lineup, slowed by gossiping residents in no hurry to get back to their lives.

"People always felt equal here, whether rich or poor, property owners or tenants," she continued, while the younger woman listened, eager to absorb the stories of her new island home. "People depend on each other for basic services and survival. Skills are often more important than income. Everybody gets to vote on island issues. We never had a sense of a divide between the Haves and Have-nots. Until this issue arose."

"So what happened?" asked the Professor's wife, choosing a cinnamon bun from the tray on the café counter. Her companion declined a bun. Too many calories. She added more sugar to her coffee.

"We did what we always do," said the older resident. "We held a public meeting in the Community Hall. Everybody gets to talk. Sometimes a decision is made. Sometimes not. So then we hold another meeting. That's why it took ten years to develop our Community Plan."

The Professor's wife had already learned that the Community Hall was the heartbeat of the island community. Located a short walk uphill from the government wharf in an era when the sea was the main transport between the islands, it was a plain, rectangular building sheathed in cedar siding with a shingled roof. Various additions had been tacked on over the years to provide communal kitchen facilities and a lounge with a bar and a fireplace with fresh kindling piled on its hearth, despite the fact that the Hall regularly failed its building code inspections. It also sheltered the community cat, which served as a rodent control officer.

"But the Hall is also the community battleground," continued the Church Warden's wife, finally relenting and reaching for an iced cinnamon bun, slathering it with butter.

"Some terrible fights there have raised the roof. None more so than the battle for the beach.

"Other issues in the past involved community disputes over land use conflicts," she explained. "The community versus the land developers. Concerns over density demands, or the number of houses that could be developed on a parcel of land. Vacation cottages versus the bed and breakfast operators. Even fights between warring factions of the same families were fought on the neutral ground of the Hall's oak floors.

"But the ugliest aspect of the battle for the beach was the split within the community between those with waterfront properties and those who did not and would never have the money to buy them. Now, for the first time, some islanders were deemed inferior to others, and began to believe the shame of it."

She paused to check the post office lineup, now down to the Old Man, a bachelor who lived alone in the valley, arguing about the cost of stamps. He liked to hear the sound of his own voice; he had no one to talk to but his dogs. The women collected their things, returned the empty coffee cups to the counter, and hastened over to the post office before it closed for lunch. The story of the battle for the beach could wait.

This is what happened, the newcomer learned later:

The public meeting was called on a weekend after the morning ferry docked to accommodate the off-islanders who wished to attend. It was chaired by the elected district politician who sat behind a table in front of the stage, facing the audience, flanked by other tables for the recording secretary and people who wished to speak. Above the stage a wooden sign displayed the words to "O Canada."

The audience sat in a circle of chairs set out in the Hall, cooled by large circulating fans hanging from the ceiling. At the end of the meeting, people would pick up and restack the chairs in the Hall foyer, clearing the room in a matter of minutes. Urns of coffee and tea, cups, and sugar and cream containers prepared by the Women's Club were set out on the tables at the back of the Hall. People streamed in.

When the last of the stragglers had butted their cigarettes in the roadway outside the door and had taken their seats, the politician called the public meeting to order and carefully explained that the public's access to public beaches was the law, and that fact was not in dispute. Some members of the audience frowned and pushed their chairs back, making a screeching sound on the oak floor to mark their displeasure. Others smiled their approval. She turned the mic over to the Chair of Parks and Recreation, with obvious relief, and sat down.

The Chair flipped open his laptop and turned on his PowerPoint presentation, unleashing a wave of music and pictures of sunlit forest trails and stone-strewn beaches on the screen mounted on the stage. A map of the island showing small black lines radiating inland from the shoreline displayed the surveyed public right-of-ways that had not yet been developed to allow the public to use them, he explained.

But not all of them were suitable for public access, he added, highlighting a line marked on the screen with his laser pointer. Some routes ended abruptly at the edge of a steep cliff, or were laid through a jumble of rocks. These were too dangerous to develop. Scenes of rocky barricades and horrific bluffs rising out of the sea, pounded by punishing waves, appeared on the screen. The music swelled with an alarming crescendo of strings punctuated by violent blats from brass trombones and trumpets.

"The Parks Committee has identified possibly twenty routes that can be safely cleared and marked for use by the public," the Chair said. The music ebbed to sweet murmurs while the screen showed scenes of leafy trails, covered with wood chips, meandering through the forests and ending in steps to a shell-covered beach. He closed his laptop and said, "Now we would like to hear from you."

Well! People rose from their seats and jostled for position in the lineup at the microphone positioned in front of the audience. When the pushing and shoving became unruly, the recording secretary, hired for the occasion by the local politician, recorded names on a speakers' list. "Each speaker has three minutes to make their comments," she told them. No one paid attention.

The barrage began. The first speaker, a retired land surveyor, outlined the provincial legislation governing public access and claimed the meeting was unnecessary since the issue was the law of the land. Boring, signaled the crowd. The Chair politely cut him off.

The second, a scruffy young man, stuck his hands in his well-worn jeans, scuffed his muddy boots on the oak floor, and said he was against the public access proposal since it would mean more people would trespass on places they shouldn't be.

Like his pot patch, snickered the audience. The police had stopped the young man's truck at the terminal on the Big Island as it drove off the ferry with a load of fragrant, freshly harvested weed in the back. He had no idea how it had got there, the young driver told them. The load was confiscated. No charges were laid.

The audience was less tolerant of the next speaker, a local land developer. He spoke movingly of his love for the island and its private spaces that would be desecrated with cigarette butts, plastic bottles, and sandwich wraps by people walking the public accesses to the beach.

His listeners rolled their eyes. A few booed. No one on island made more money by rezoning parcels of rural land into smaller, expensive residential lots, in return for dedicating strips of land for public access. These strips were usually rocky wastes, which would never pass a soil test for septic tanks, and thus could never be developed for houses.

A tiny, white haired woman spoke in favour of the program, arguing that well marked, cleared public accesses would show people where they were welcome and where they were not, reducing the threat of trespassers. "Good point," some members of the audience murmured.

The debate boiled over into heated exchanges. An off-islander opposed development of an access trail leading to a popular swimming beach since the plan showed the Parks Committee would install outdoor composting toilets on the site that was adjacent to his waterfront home.

"Would you prefer people peeing in the bushes and pooping on the sand?" someone called out from the audience. "Or festooning the blackberry bushes with used toilet paper?"

An American couple argued liability issues. "Who would be responsible if people on the beach broke their ankle or their legs on the rocky shoreline in front of their homes?" The crowd snorted. People broke bones on the beach all the time, climbing in and out of boats, hauling them out of the water. The couple was known to have chased visitors off the beach in front of their house, threatening to sue them for trespassing.

A weekender stood up and complained that since no one ever used the access that paralleled his property line down to the beach, he didn't see why it should be cleared and marked. Duh! Some of his listeners rolled their eyes.

Another said he didn't want the riff-raff near his property because they might leave the fences open so the pasturing sheep could escape. Someone in the audience pointed out the island sheep wandered at will along the roads, grazing the grass lining the local ditches.

A big beefy man lumbered to his feet and said that allowing people to roam the island, particularly his section, increased the risk of forest fires. A ripple of resentment swept the room. "He's from Fascist Estates, a gated community guarded with NO TRESPASSING signs plastered over the entrance," whispered an old-timer to his neighbour. Everybody knew some of the property owners—even the armchair socialists—had built their houses over the perimeter trails, excluding the public from enjoying the cliff-side views of the Sound.

The tone of the debate turned ugly. Someone accused his neighbour of building his garage on public land, a charge hotly denied by the irate victim. Others charged that the local orchardist had stolen public property by planting his trees right across the public access and fencing the land off with locked gates.

When one woman pulled out her handkerchief and mopped her tears, claiming she would fear for her life if she found strangers on her beach, and would need to sleep with a gun under her pillow, someone yelled, "Then go back where you came from!" Probably Montana. Or Texas. Gun country.

The air grew rancid with acrimony and the smell of cigarette smoke from those in the audience who had withdrawn to the porch. The ladies of the Women's Club rose from their seats and headed for the kitchen to make coffee and tea and to reward the community cat with food in payment for mousing duties. The Chair banged the gavel and adjourned the meeting so some folks could leave on the ferry to the Mainland.

To an observer, the issue would appear to have been unresolved. But as the cauldron of island debate cooled, a consensus congealed in the conversations over the bridge table, in the pub, and around the coffee table in the café, the "car bar" at the community's garage where people shared their six-packs with their friends amid the rusting wrecks of abandoned island vehicles.

The law was the law. Those who chose to live beside a public access had the public as their neighbours. And the beaches belonged to everyone.

And so, over time and by stealth, the Parks Committee volunteers cleared some of the trails and marked their entrances. They circulated notices to the nearest neighbours, soliciting their help and dealing with their concerns, but they did not retreat. Over the years, they endured endless field trips from bureaucrats who passed the file around to their colleagues in different offices in other regions, often burying them until forced to dig them out after calls and letters to politicians.

After a time, people became accustomed to the trails, even taking them for granted, swinging through the trees and down the slopes in their Tilley hats and hiking boots, wielding their Nordic poles, drawing the forest-scented air deep into their city-parched lungs, gingerly side-stepping the fresh horse dung steaming on the wood chips covering the paths, stopping to enjoy the views and to watch the wheeling ospreys and eagles gliding down the wind thermals, and furtively stuffing a chocolate lily or other plant specimen into their back packs in defiance of Park rules.

People sat on the wooden benches and spread their sandwiches on the tables set up at the trail's end. Children and dogs swam in the cold waters lapping the stone-pebbled beaches and hunted for marine life—barnacles, mussels, and the odd oyster—along the shores. No home invasions or duct-taped victims were reported.

Sometimes the Church Warden's wife drove out to the battleground and sat on the bench, watching the sun rise over the mountains on the Mainland, listening for the snort of a sea lion, or waiting for the mists to clear over the neighbouring islands, revealing their beauty. Peace seemed restored to the island.

Until the public access signs, with their stick figures swinging Nordic poles, started disappearing.

When he first learned of the thefts, the Chair thought it was the work of young vandals. His volunteers replaced the signs, bending the bolts so they would be harder to dislodge. But then the perp splashed the markers with solvent and peeled the signs off.

Not the work of vandals out for fun.

Someone noted that the damage occurred only after long weekends, when off-islanders returned. His crew grimly replaced them. Posters were printed and posted, asking for information.

People were uneasy.

Then new signs went up on the bulletin board in the General Store:

CRIME ALERT
SOMEONE IS STEALING WATER
FROM THE CISTERNS
IF YOU HAVE ANY INFORMATION
ON THE PERSONS RESPONSIBLE
PLEASE CALL THE RCMP
REWARD WILL BE PAID

MEDICAL CLINIC

THE CHURCH WARDEN'S WIFE PRIDED herself on her perfect health. For her age, of course. Except for the arthritis that left her a bit stiff in the mornings. Then there was the fact that people seemed to talk more softly in her presence. Sometimes she couldn't follow the conversation at the Women's Club meetings.

Her husband assured her she was healthy enough to cater to his needs and wants. When she gingerly unfolded herself from her chair to feed the cat he would ask from his reclining chair, where he sat reading the *Salish Sounder* newspaper, "While you are up, old girl, you might as well get me another coffee." He complained of shortness of breath.

Still, she was cheerfully optimistic when she walked up to the island medical clinic to see the nurse practitioner for her annual checkup. The NP came by water taxi every Tuesday from the neighbouring island. The doctor from the Big

Island was available between morning and afternoon ferries on Wednesday. On Thursday, a community nurse from off island held a clinic from mid-morning until noon.

Islanders requiring medical services the rest of the week depended on the Emergency Services volunteers, who trained at the Fire Hall and transported the sick by water taxi or helicopter as needed. Most times it seemed to work. Few people actually died on island, although her own mother did, the Church Warden's wife reflected, trudging up the gravel road, edged with yellow gorse and dust-covered blackberry bushes, to the clinic.

When her father died, her widowed mother moved to the island to be near her daughter, bringing her husband's ashes with her in a small urn. After several uneventful years, she was helicoptered off the island following a heart attack.

"It was my first helicopter ride," she told her daughter, who was off island at the time. "They took me down to the schoolyard and strapped me into the helicopter and we lifted up into the air and over the sea to the hospital. It was very exciting, darling. BUT!" She held onto her daughter's arthritic hands. "I don't want to do it again."

And she didn't.

The medical clinic also offered a variety of other medical or alternative medical services, including regular massage therapy, occasional visits by an off-island physiotherapist and an audio specialist, and an eclectic mix of exercise programs with yoga, stretching, qigong, karate, and walking programs offered by island volunteers of various expertise, ranging from excellent to non-existent.

The medical clinic was attached to the community's indoor basketball court. The registered massage therapist aroused the ire of the local basketball players by shutting down their games every weekend when she set up her massage table. "The thumping and bumping disturbs my patients," she told them crossly as they dribbled the basketball despondently back to the games locker.

All these activities were guaranteed to keep island hearts pumping, or at least pounding, as islanders puffed their way along the gravel roads and mountain trails wielding their Nordic poles. According to the local health committee's statistics, the average age of the islanders was substantially older than those on the Big Island.

The Church Warden no longer attended the medical clinic. He became embroiled in a feud with the local garage owner who had offered the attic space over his grease-stained garage to the community as the island's original clinic. For years the islanders had made their way past the car wrecks and cannibalized trucks and the "car bar," with its dedicated drinkers, and climbed the stairs to the ant-infested rooms above, bandages and splints spilling off the shelves.

To mark his gift of the attic space, the garage owner inscribed his name on a plaque and hung it over the dilapidated clinic door. When the community, pushed by the health authorities, built the new clinic the garage owner moved his sign to the new building and grandly nailed it above the freshly installed door. A few nights later the sign disappeared.

This act of vandalism was widely attributed to the Church Warden, who had publicly preached that many in the community had contributed funds and sweat equity to the new clinic, including the local service club, in which he served as past president, and that the garage owner's name plate did not deserve to be hung at the new site.

The islanders were divided on the issue, some dismayed and others delighted. The merits of the signage and its theft were much discussed in the "car bar" and coffee shop, and Saturday night sauna at the sheep farm, and in the columns of the weekly paper.

When the sign was found stashed in the pile of old tires behind the garage, the owner hauled it back to the clinic and pounded it into place above the door. A few nights later it had vanished again, and was subsequently found behind the Fire Hall. Again, the garage owner trucked the sign back to the clinic, climbed up his ladder and reinstalled his plaque, only to find it was removed under the cover of dark.

Eventually, the Church Warden tired of his vigilante role and avoided the clinic, taking the ferry to town for his blood pressure readings. When the garage owner died and passed on to the Great Car Bar in the Sky, no one bothered to remove the disputed sign.

When she arrived at the clinic, the Church Warden's wife

glanced up and noted that the garage owner's sign was firmly fastened in its place above the entry door. As she waited her turn with the nurse practitioner, she shared her hearing problems with other patients slouched in the clinic chairs, who gossiped about their neighbours' health issues and readily recounted their ailments, real or imagined, beneath the sign posted on the clinic wall that proclaimed:

YOUR MEDICAL RECORDS ARE CONFIDENTIAL TO YOU AND YOUR PERSONAL PHYSICIANS HOWEVER IT IS ACCEPTED THAT MEDICAL INFORMATION MAY BE SHARED AMONG PHYSICIANS DIRECTLY INVOLVED IN YOUR CARE

And with most of the neighbours, reflected the Church Warden's wife.

Other notices posted on the walls or mounted on the clinic's counter gave tips on PREVENTING FALLS: A SERIOUS CASE OF FATALITIES AMONG SENIORS, a HELP LINE telephone number FOR SPOUSAL ABUSE, and a warning that ABUSIVE LANGUAGE AND ABUSIVE OUTBURSTS WILL NOT BE TOLERATED BY STAFF.

Outside, the island's ancient ambulance rolled up to the medical clinic's glass door and a volunteer driver climbed down, slamming the vehicle's door so hard it rocked both the ambulance and the windows of the clinic. "Shit," said the driver. "The Old Man is done for this time. Broke his hip again walking the dog. We just strapped his stretcher into the helicopter for the flight to town."

There were concerned bleats from the clinic crowd, who could hear the *whump-whump* of the helicopter as it roared over the roof of the medical clinic. The Old Man was pushing 100 years old and had endured a number of fractures, falling off his tractor, skidding off his barn roof, rear-ending his old Ford—which he drove until he was ninety-five years old, stubbornly repeating his driving test until the exasperated examiner renewed his licence, warning him to stay on the island's gravel roads and off the Big Island's major highway.

The wife left her neighbours in the waiting room debating the Old Man's odds, which were poor. "I am perfectly healthy," she told the nurse practitioner when she was finally ushered into the small room with its examining table, desk, two chairs, and a weigh scale. The windows were open. The clinic was financed by community picnics and barbeques and the budget did not stretch to air conditioning.

She sat down facing the nurse practitioner and explained about her hearing problems, and the nurse practitioner peered into her ears with a cold instrument. "It's just wax buildup," said the NP briskly. She was an ample woman with an amiable manner who had won her patients' trust. She picked up her pen and opened the file on her desk. "Now let's look at your blood work. Good. It is all within range."

"I told you I am perfectly fine," said the wife, relieved. A common worry among islanders was failing health, and possible commitment to the old-age home in town. "Except of course for my two artificial hips. And now I have a new artificial knee. It still feels swollen and hurts a bit."

"That's what Tylenol is for," said the NP. She updated the information about total joint replacements and swollen knees in her file. "Now let's review your prescriptions." She picked up another paper from the file.

It was a rather long list: medications for arthritis, blood pressure, and thyroid, as well as heart medicine, water pills, painkillers, and vitamins—the basic medical kit of any healthy senior.

The process of filling the prescription needs of islanders was a bit complicated. First the medical practitioner faxed the prescription to the pharmacy on the Big Island. Then the patient phoned the pharmacy to give a credit card number. The prescription was placed in the island basket on the pharmacy counter and picked up once a week by a volunteer on the way to the ferry.

Back on island the volunteer left the basket at the General Store, or, in case of closure, the pub or the Wharf Store, and the patient was phoned and advised to come and pick it up. In the rare case of system breakdown, the ferry attendant was known to deliver the prescription personally if it was on her way home from work. Few people died on island of a drug overdose, unless alcohol is classified as a drug, reflected the NP.

At the medical clinic the NP tapped the wife's joints with

a rubber hammer. "Ouch," said her patient, rubbing her sore knees. "You know I don't have any rotator muscle left in my shoulder and I can't lift my right arm above the waist." The NP wrote that down in the file too.

"How is your appetite? Do you eat properly?" she asked.

"I can eat anything," said her patient. "Except of course anything with fat. Since I had my gall bladder removed I throw up fatty foods."

The NP again entered that information in the file and asked, "Have you had a hysterectomy?"

"No," said her patient. "I've just had my ovaries removed."

The NP paused in her examination of the wife's surgically scarred body. "Are you sure?" she asked.

"Yes," replied the wife, struggling into her clothes, hampered by her crippled arm.

"Is that all?" the NP persisted, who knew the islanders' reluctance to admit to any disability or disease that might result in a recommendation to move off island, closer to medical services.

The wife looked at her anxiously. When did the fearlessness of youth become the fearful descent into old age, she thought, when the slightest crack in the pattern of daily life triggered a seismic shift of panic? When a DETOUR sign on the highway was terrifying, taking her into uncharted territory of unfamiliar neighbourhoods? When she learned her doctor had moved his office a block away, she collapsed in floods of tears—where would she park?

"I'm fine," she said. "The last bad thing that happened to me was this winter when my husband was away and I was watching TV and stood up too fast and fell and cut arteries in my scalp and passed out and phoned 911 when I came to and the volunteers arrived and ordered the helicopter and I was transported to Big Island General emergency where the doctors said I had lost three pints of blood and almost died!"

She paused for breath, remembering how her mother died in her own bed in her own house with her own dog for company and friends nearby, her will neatly placed in the drawer of her bedside table where it would be easily found. Her ashes were buried beside her husband's urn in the island cemetery on the road past the garage.

Her thoughts returned to the present as the nurse practitioner put away her stethoscope, closed the file, put down her pen, and turned in her chair to face the wife. "You are right," she smiled. "You passed your checkup with flying colours. You are perfectly healthy. For your age!"

BURN PILE

AMONG THE CHORES OF ISLAND living, the task of supplying the newcomers' wood-burning cook stove with paper, kindling, and chopped wood was central. In winter, the cook stove was their supplementary source of heat, augmenting the thin output of the electrical baseboard heaters that lined the walls of the house, and creating the toasty warmth that only wood-burning stoves can supply.

In honor of its role, the Professor and his wife called their coal-black and steel-filigreed stove, with its oven and commodious warming shelf, Cook.

When power outages occurred Cook became essential, heating the house, cooking the food, warming the water in the large tin kettle for hand and dishwashing, its firebox offering a splash of firelight in the winter dark. Cook was a great source of comfort in a cold winter.

Cook's weakness was the need for paper to kindle her

firebox. Wood and kindling were no problem since clearing the road right-of-ways and storm windfalls supplied an unending source for the local service club to chop and sell.

But paper was scarce. Few newspapers made their way to the island and most were routinely returned to the Recycling Centre. Even paper envelopes from island mail were readdressed and posted to local residents in the Free Mail rack in the General Store.

The paper source of last resource was the burn pile, located at the site of the small island sawmill that processed island timber. The sawmill was located up the mountain, a short distance from the General Store, which served, along with the Fire Hall and Recycling Centre, as the town centre.

The burn pile was the crematorium for all combustibles deemed beyond any value or use: old timber; slabs of bark; boards from abandoned cabins; tree trimmings unsuitable for the chipper that created the mulch used for garden paths; frayed news clippings; the debris and detritus of lives no longer lived.

The Professor's wife drove her hatchback up the single-lane road on a sunny, chilly day when frost iced the rooftops and fields in the valley. She passed the yellow and black road sign showing a logging truck heading downhill—a warning—and turned left onto a rugged, rutted road, torn up by trucks turning, and parked near a gang of old trucks, windows broken, doors hanging loose. One gaunt, mottled flat-deck looked like it had been pulled out of the ocean down by the landing where logs were dumped into the water.

She opened the door of the car and stepped down onto the black mud, ice still bridging the ruts, and adjusted the knot on the kerchief that covered her hair. She had dressed for this, pants stuffed into the tops of her rubber boots, the sleeves of her wind jacket pulled down her wrists to meet her gloved hands.

Using her Hawthorne walking stick to steady herself, she stepped over slippery ends of two-by-fours soaking in the muddy ruts, avoiding the thorns of the gorse bushes stiffened by the cold, and headed for the burn pile to see what paper she could salvage to satisfy Cook. Crows stalked the tin roof of the sawmill, cawing as two men welded some machine in the dark cavern below.

She waved her stick at them and then pointed it at the burn pile to indicate her intentions. The sawmill operator pushed back his welder's shield and nodded okay. Then, changing his mind, he came down the hill to talk to her. "Let me give you a hand," he said. "It's pretty slippery down there."

She took his arm, breathing in the warm, sweaty smell of his fleece vest. "I'm looking for paper to light the cook stove," she explained. "The freight truck has taken recycling to town."

"You're in luck," he replied, navigating them past a crumpled pile of galvanized tin roof. "We just got a load from the valley, when the relatives took the Old Man to the nursing home." The sawmill operator named a long-time bachelor who had lived alone. "I don't really like handling this stuff," he added. "It's pretty personal. And some of it is really weird. You may not like what you find." He positioned her in a safe spot beside the burn pile and returned up the hill to his welder's cave.

The burn pile was beside a deep ash-filled pit where the actual burning took place in compliance with local regulations. Use of the pit and the burning was monitored by local volunteer firemen, alerted when the columns of smoke from the pit spiraled above the surrounding forest.

She skirted the pit with care, scouting the edges of the burn pile, looking for random sources of burnable paper. She found some clippings chronicling local events from the island's weekly newspaper, some legal papers, catalogues with pages cut out, old technical papers, stuffing them into her cloth grocery bag stamped with the Save the Whales logo. She felt happy, useful, pleased with herself and her thrifty housewifery, enjoying the clean air, the sun warming her face.

Then she spotted a scribble on a scrap of paper by her boot. She stooped to extract the scrap from the pile and smoothed out the wrinkles. The writing was shaky and off-kilter, angled across the page. She read:

> *I am consumed by him.*
> *I am consumed by what he did to me, to my relationships, to other people.*
> *Why can't I let go?????*

She was struck by the anguish implicit in the scrawled message. And then curious. Who had written it? To whom was it addressed? She turned the paper over in her hands, seeking clues to the writer's identity. She did not recognize the handwriting. But that was not surprising in the current culture of emails and Facebook. Who wrote notes to anyone anymore?

She stood in the cold sunshine, the frost still shining in the bark of the abandoned slabs of timber, and thought. The only material consigned to the burn pile was the debris of the dead, the deserted, old people carted off to the old-age homes on the Big Island, material deemed useless to the heirs and caregivers, or too embarrassing to retain in family records.

So who among the island population had died recently, or moved, or downsized? The Old Man did not seem a likely source; the author sounded like a woman. Nobody else came to mind. She stirred the edges of the burn pile with her walking stick, seeking similar scraps and then stopped, enveloped by a slow sense of shame, a voyeur of another person's pain.

She stuffed the scrap of paper into her cloth bag along with her other scavenged treasures and returned to her small hatchback, heaving the bag onto the back seat. She drove carefully home down the mountain road, avoiding the worst of the black ice.

At least Cook would be happy.

It was some time before the wife returned to the burn pile. The off-island chimney sweep had descended on his broom, whipping through the island homes between ferries, and had decried Cook as not to code: TOO CLOSE TO COMBUSTIBLE MATERIAL. He left a note on her black stovetop: DO NOT USE THIS STOVE. In the rhythm of island life, it took time to snag the local chimney expert to restore Cook to insurable status and reduce the shivers endured by the now heavily sweatered couple.

Winter was on the wane when the wife returned to the burn pile. Nothing much had changed. The ground was still muddy, although the ice had melted. Once again she waved to the sawmill operator, moving junk around with his loader, and picked her way over to the burn pit.

She refused to admit to herself that she was looking for more information from the anonymous author of the despairing note. Her heart quickened when her stick unearthed a Valentine card, which featured two coy sheep. The male sheep was saying in his balloon script, "I woolly yarn for ewe." The female, identified by a ribbon in her collar, replied, in her heart-shaped balloon, "Flock off!"

The wife smiled. She recognized the work of a local artist famous for her kooky work. She also recognized the handwriting of the inscription, which said simply, "your loving wife" in the same script recorded on the scribbled note salvaged earlier. There was no other clue to the writer's identity.

It was on her third trip to the burn pile that she unearthed tatters of correspondence that rang alarm bells in her head.

This time the crumpled ball of paper appeared to be a series of emails, torn and ripped, in no particular sequence. The addresses were cute code names, not likely to be found in the island directory.

She peeled the first one from the clump she had retrieved from the edges of the burn pile.

> *No one has ever threatened you with anything. One jest does not a murder make. What I said was "you have no throttle." To suggest that it meant I would abuse you is as patently ridiculous as the rest of your fantasies. Have another drinkypoo.*

A death threat? She scrabbled through the soggy sheets of paper to find the original message. She found a possible one.

> *I take you at your word. And your word at the supper table was "you should be throttled." Rewrite it any way you want. It is not acceptable in civil society.*

Concern coursed through her body. She scanned the other pages clutched in her ungloved hands, seeking to make some sense of the correspondence, to identify who was at risk. She read:

> *Over the last three weeks I have considered leaving this life . . . and to end this mental pain. I can't*

think of a way to end this life without leaving a
mess behind.

Suicide? Shouldn't she tell someone? But the address was blurred. Was this a depressed husband or an abused wife? She couldn't tell. She pulled out another sheet.

. . . the credit card was mine as well as yours.
Don't make it look fraudulent. The household
cheques were an honest account error . . . I simply
ran out of money while the accounts were being
transferred. Simple.

Fraudulent? She gingerly separated another sheet.

. . . I don't understand your approach to mar-
riage either but mine does not include a husband
who tells another woman he loves her very much
while he tells his wife to fuck off. IT IS NOT
REASONABLE FOR A WIFE TO SHARE A
BED WITH HER HUSBAND UNDER THOSE
CIRCUMSTANCES. It is simply not acceptable, a
view I think is generally held.

Shades of Jane Austen! But adultery, well, that was more plausible in island society. She was constantly bewildered by the number of couplings and un-couplings that took place on island. Sometimes she felt she could hardly keep up with the comings and goings among the residents, let alone the summer people.

That night, in bed, she listened to her husband snuffling and snoring beside her. When he got up to pee for the third time she left the bed and crawled between the sheets in the guest room. Their chocolate-eared cat followed her. Who could this unhappy, warring couple be?

She thought about her own marriage. In their more affectionate moments she called her husband Hubby-Dubby. She couldn't imagine Hubby-Dubby leaving her for another woman.

But who knew what went on in a relationship except those actually in it? She wondered if Hubby-Dubby was even aware she had left his bed. Or if he missed the cat. She turned over in bed and finally fell asleep.

She did not use the emails she had found in the burn pile to light Cook. Instead she sealed them in a recycled brown envelope and buried them in her desk drawer, until the thought occurred to her that when the time came for her private papers to go to the burn pile, her family would think the exchange of emails was between her and Hubby-Dubby. She deposited them between her cookbooks instead.

Over the summer, she listened to her neighbours more carefully than ever before, seeking clues to the unhappy couple's identity. She listened in church, normally the source of most of her information on whose cancer had returned, whose brother had died, whose grandchildren had mumps. There was very little Good News in church, she reflected, no matter what the Bible said.

She took to stopping for morning coffee at the café, which she never had done, to share the island gossip. In her case she had little to contribute but she learned a lot, but nothing that pointed to the identity of the couple. On the ferry to town she scrutinized the faces of the people sitting in their cars, seeking those who sat together in stoic but companionable silence, or reading their library books, and who were snapping like turtles at each other.

She listened at bridge to interminable complaints, accusations, innuendos, and grievances as the cards were dealt and studied and teacups filled. At the medical clinic she wrote down the numbers for the Violence Against Women hotline and worried about spousal abuse, the verbal and non-verbal kind.

Her silence earned her a reputation as a woman of depth. But she learned nothing about the couple whose secrets were buried in the burn pile.

Then one autumn night when she was playing her favourite Joni Mitchell songs on her piano, singing along softly, enjoying a peaceful evening while Hubby-Dubby was attending a meeting of the Men's Club, the telephone rang. Irritated, she closed her songbook and picked up the phone. "Hello?" she snapped.

On the line a woman sobbed. A woman she hardly knew,

who lived on the Gulf side. A woman she probably wouldn't recognize if they encountered each other off island, and whose husband she had never met.

"I don't know who else to call," the woman sobbed. "You are so discreet. You never say anything. But I think my husband is going to leave me and I don't know what to do." Between sniffles and wails she described how she had picked up her husband's cell phone and there was a text message about a green coat—she didn't own a green coat—that had been left in her husband's car and needed to be returned.

"We've been married all these years and I never really thought he would cheat on me, that he would take up with somebody else. It is not acceptable in civil society." The distraught woman rambled on while the wife, stunned into silence, did what she did best, just listened, murmuring "my, my," and "goodness, did he really?" and that soothing, useless "now, now," realizing from the sobbing woman's story that she was hearing first-hand from the heroine of her burn pile drama.

It's not acceptable in civil society.

If *heroine* was the word. Maybe *victim* was a better one. Either way, the anguish was as genuine as the words scribbled on the pieces of paper hidden among her cookbooks.

The listener on the phone was engulfed in remorse. She wanted to say *I know the pain you have endured. I know about*

the missing money, the possible suicide/murder threats. I read the
emails but I am too ashamed to admit it. I don't know the woman
in the green coat. I would tell you if I did. But I didn't know who
you were, who to go to for help.

But she couldn't find her voice, couldn't get past the fear that closed her throat.

What would happen to her caller? How would this saga end?

Finally the tearful woman slowed down, exhausted, her words halting, ending with a whispered "Don't tell anyone about this."

"I won't," the wife whispered back. "No one. Not a soul."

And she never did. Nor did she go back to the burn pile for paper to feed Cook. Instead, she took the emails down from the cookbooks and burned them. Some secrets should go up in smoke.

FISH FRY

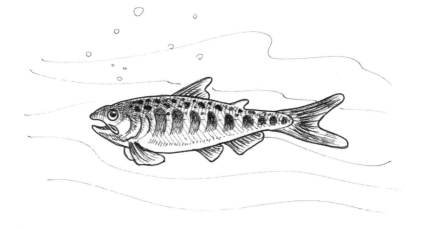

THE PROFESSOR SAT AT HIS desk in his book-lined den and turned off his laptop. He swivelled in his ergonomic chair and gazed glumly out the window at the rockery of native plants, imported from town, that the island deer so enjoyed grazing day and night. A regular buffet, he thought. And an expensive one.

He yawned.

He was bored, he admitted to himself. When he was coaxed by his wife to leave town and move to the island he had no idea there would be so little to do. There was no golf course. No faculty club. No retired lawyers' lunches. Only the local newspaper delivered by the mail boat. He could access the national and regional newspapers online, but he found he was increasingly uninterested in what happened on the Mainland.

And the *silence*, alternating with the lack of it. The croak of the heron fishing before dawn. The irritating caw of the crows. The amplified voice of the ferry captain over the loud-speaker announcing the ship's imminent arrival at the dock. The drone of the float planes and the powerboats on the sea beyond the cottage.

Outside, the white cat with the chocolate ears prowled through the rockery, chewing stalks of grass. She'll throw up on the carpet later, the Professor thought sourly.

He swung around in his chair and reviewed his book-shelves. Maybe he should write a book. Brightening, he swung back to his desk and rebooted his laptop, bringing up a blank page on his word processor, and considered a title. He liked writing titles. Trouble was he couldn't think of stories to go with them.

He typed *Ride the Dead Horses*, inspired by a memory from his youth, when he and his older brother mounted the dead steeds in the anatomy lab of the veterinary college where his father taught. He remembered the cold, slippery hair on the horses, strung up by wires attached to the walls and ceiling of the lab. His nostrils constricted with the memory of the smell of formaldehyde injected into the horses to preserve them.

But then his mind went blank.

Think of all those cases of spousal abuse in my files, he reminded himself. Surely there is useful material there. Could be therapeutic for some couples, maybe save some marriages. Those books make real money. He typed *Body Blows*.

On second thought, he realized, those files represent client-solicitor confidences. His former clients might sue him. He highlighted *Body Blows* and pressed the delete button. After typing *Big Bad Wolf: A History of Criminals Whom the Courts Found Innocent,* he sighed and pressed the delete button again. He turned off his computer, grabbed his hoodie, and left to meet his wife at the annual island salmon barbeque in the community park.

He drove past the Recycling Centre. The sign on the Free Store declared IF WE DON'T HAVE IT YOU DON'T WANT IT. The road to the park passed the local marina, where the sign on the boathouse read IF YOU HAVE NOTHING TO DO DON'T DO IT HERE.

The island thrives on negativity, he thought. The sign on the ferry dock set the tone for visitors, with the warning BEWARE OF SHIP'S PROPELLERS. KEEP CLEAR AT ALL TIMES SWIMMING FISHING AND SCUBA DIVING PROHIBITED. The sign might as well have proclaimed KEEP OUT.

He parked under the trees at the park and searched for his wife. Raised in a small town, she had taken to island life more easily than he had, sorting clothes at the Free Store, contributing her social worker skills to the local clinic's health committee, singing in the community choir.

He, on the other hand, hadn't made many friends on the island. He was slight in stature, unfit for volunteer fireman or emergency response duties. He didn't know how to run a power saw or chop wood, so he was useless to the service club firewood crew. He didn't do karate or qigong at the recreation centre.

He found his wife at the park pavilion, serving up salad to the islanders lined up for lunch. He took his plate of grilled salmon, salad, and a buttered bun, picked up a knife and fork wrapped in a napkin, and sat down at one of the picnic tables next to the Church Warden, who was busily filling his mouth with food, his napkin tucked into his shirt front.

The Church Warden looked warily at the newcomer sitting beside him. The tension between the two reflected the invisible tug-of-war that existed between the old, established island families and those new to island ways. The newcomers sometimes challenged the old-timers with newfangled ideas and activities. Like karate and qigong. And rarely went to church, except for memorial services and Christmas carol singing.

The Professor wasn't an atheist. At least, not quite. Occasionally he and his wife attended interdenominational services in the church. They both knew they would never live long enough to be granted island citizenship. Their cottage would always be known by the name of the family who built it decades ago, not by their own family name.

The old-timers and the newcomers even had different names for different island features, such as the hills and bays. The old-timers referred to them by the names of the pioneers who lived there, while the newcomers used the names on the maps. Sometimes tourists seeking directions were caught in the cultural crossfire.

At the front of the pavilion, a middle-aged man was giving a report on the community's efforts to restock the local salmon stream. His audience listened intently while munching lunch.

"How did that come about?" the Professor asked the Church Warden, intrigued that such a small community could successfully undertake such a huge effort. "Who is the speaker?"

The Church Warden pulled his napkin out of his collar, wiped his mouth, and straightened his fork and knife on his plate. He loved to tell new islanders about island history. Maybe this hapless urban retiree wasn't as insignificant as he seemed.

"That's our local tour operator. Takes the tourists out in his whale boat to see the orcas and the eagles and the kelp beds," the Warden said. "Used to be a carpenter. Bit of a roustabout then, our lad. First to down tools at the job site, last to leave the pub at closing time. Good ball player, but restless. Fought with his girlfriend."

The Warden warmed up to his topic.

One day, he continued, the young man stopped by the elementary school to use the phone—his girlfriend was the teacher—and noticed chum salmon fry swimming in the aquarium in the two-room schoolhouse.

The students fed the fry over the winter school term,

the teacher explained. The kids gave names to each fry. In the spring, she would take her students to the nearby tidal creek to release the fry in the hopes they would return to the creek four years later.

Why bother? the young man asked the teacher. Everybody knew the creek was dead. Once it was a salmon spawning stream for chum, coho, even chinook. But that was before the timbered road bridge collapsed into the creek, tearing out the banks, plugging the stream, trapping the spawning salmon upstream of the road bridge

Back then the road crew replaced the bridge with a steel culvert, the Church Warden related. But the diameter of the culvert was too small for the returning salmon to swim through to reach the spawning grounds upstream, too small for the young fry to swim back out the following spring when the flooding tides at the mouth of the creek would sweep them out to sea.

"So the creek died," the Warden said. "The Old Man, who lived in the cabin that backed onto the creek, said he hadn't seen a chum or a sea trout in the stream for years. But that is not the end of the story."

"The story of the coast," said the Professor ruefully, finishing his blackberry pie. So many salmon spawning streams had been destroyed by the construction of logging roads near creek beds, log dumps in the estuaries, boat launches, sea walls, housing developments, and other man-made incursions threatening the coastal salmon runs so vital to coastal communities.

He rose from the table, collected two cups of coffee from the urns at the back of the pavilion, elbowed his way through the lineup of people waiting for their share of succulent salmon, and returned to the picnic table. "Please go on," he said. The old boy is pretty interesting, he thought.

Only too pleased to do so, the Warden continued. "Our young lad decided that the answer was pretty simple. Replace the culvert with a bigger one and the salmon might return. It took him twenty years and generations of school kids to do it."

The government road crews did eventually install a larger diameter culvert, he said, but the silting in the creek over the years had raised the creek bed, and the steel culvert was too high for the returning chum to swim through in order to reach the spawning grounds upstream. Unlike some other salmon species, explained the Church Warden, chum can't jump.

So in late autumn, at the start of the spawning season, the young man organized a small group of islanders to save the salmon. They met with their nets and buckets at the stream below the culvert and waited for the salmon to arrive and mill about in groups of five or six in the brackish water.

Over time, they netted 600 chum salmon, each weighing up to fifteen pounds. They carried them in buckets across the road to the creek upstream of the culvert and released them to swim to the gravel spawning grounds hidden in the jungle growth of the forest.

They worked at night, hanging lanterns in the trees, to escape the ospreys and eagles and other predators who fished the creek in daylight. Then they waited to see if the salmon fry survived the winter, cheering when they wiggled downstream through the creek water in the spring.

But that was the year of the drought, the Church Warden continued. The autumn rains did not appear, and when the salmon returned to spawn, the water levels in the creek were too low for the fish to swim upstream to the spawning grounds. Instead they became food for the seals and river otters feeding in the intertidal zone at the mouth of the creek.

But the island volunteers didn't give up. The next year they collected 50,000 eggs from the Big Island hatchery and deposited them in the gravel beds of the upstream spawning grounds, adding 100,000 eggs the following year and the next. When the National Park acquired the creek, crews removed truckloads of earth to restore the stream to its original creek bed and positioned a concrete culvert at the proper elevation for the chum to swim through.

In time, salmon were seen in the creek. Some chum, a few coho, more cutthroat trout, a member of the salmon family. Hard to count how many, said the volunteer, now in his mid-forties. The returning salmon were difficult to count since they preferred muddy water to escape predators.

Each year, the school children raised about 200 baby chum in their classroom aquarium, pouring the eggs from the hatchery into the big glass tank, watching them fall among the stones on the bottom of the tank, feeding the fry as they emerged from the eggs and grew bigger.

In the spring, when the runoff raised the water levels in the creek, the teacher changed the temperature of the water in the aquarium to match the temperature of the creek water. Then, when the fry were big enough, the children carried them, still swimming, in a big bucket to the creek.

Each child had their own small container and scooped the fry out of the bucket, then crouched on the bank to release them into the creek to find their way to the sea.

"Were they sad to see them go?" asked the Church Warden rhetorically, finishing his story. "Of course not. They knew that the life cycle of the salmon would bring some of them home to the creek in a few years. Go talk to the tour operator about the work his volunteers are doing." He pushed back his plate, stood up, and looked around for his wife.

The Professor turned his coffee cup between his palms, remembering the nature walk the couple took down in the valley earlier that summer. The Park Guide arrived on her bicycle, dressed in her official khaki shirt, green shorts, and hat. She led the group—mostly tourists, including three toddlers and a teenager—down the forest path along the creek and stopped in a cool, shaded area.

"Close your eyes," instructed the Guide cheerfully. Everyone did so except the toddlers, who were picking the orange salmon berries from the bushes, squeezing them in their fists, stuffing them in their mouths.

The Professor's wife hung on to her husband's arm, remembering the couple's earlier adventure, slipping and sliding over the muddy forest floor.

"Imagine we are in a huge cathedral," said the Guide. "Take a deep breath. Now open your eyes and imagine you are taking a picture. What do you see?"

The Professor obediently opened his eyes. He saw sunlight filtering through the trees and branches, backlighting the forest floor. A cool, grassy area beside the stream, a concrete culvert peeking slyly from the bushes. A flustered mother yanking berry-stained fingers from her child's mouth. He snapped a picture with his smartphone.

The Guide pushed aside tree branches and stinging nettles and led the group across wooden bridges edged with branches, and stopped at a massive old-growth cedar stump that was nursing a young sapling. She described how a century ago the hand-loggers used wedges and planks and crosscut saws to cut the trees down.

Moss grew on the sides of the tree trunks, not only on the north side. Some branches snaked around the cedar trunks, strangling other growth. The Professor eyed the "widow makers," or branches in the forest canopy overhead poised to fall on unprotected heads.

The Guide explained how the timber and the lush ground cover were fertilized by the remains of the fish stranded in the stream when the bridge collapsed, or snared by the wild animals and seabirds during the spawning season.

"All the water in this valley comes from raindrops. There are no springs," she told them. The group clambered down an incline, carefully traversing tree roots filled with sludge, to the edge of the stream meandering through the valley floor, its muddy banks pimpled with small purple flowers among the ferns.

Here the stream narrowed to about one metre wide. The Guide told the children there were red-legged frogs in its muddy reaches, eight kinds of slugs, molluscs, snails, and creatures in shells, long-toed salamanders, rough-skinned newts. The Professor's wife remembered the sign on the General Store door warning that roads were slippery with armies of creepy crawlies in late summer.

Everyone crouched down beside the creek bed to look for salmon fry and the caddisfly larvae that hatch into flies, which the young fry eat. The Professor's wife brushed away mosquitoes as she leaned against a log that spanned the creek in the sunny, open space. She breathed in the damp smell of leaves, felt the warm sun and the cool breeze on her sweaty arms.

There were shrieks from the children when they found several fry in the creek water. Instructing them not to touch the fry, the Guide bagged and lifted some from the water. Squinting, she identified three different kinds of fish, including an inch-long fry with specks and black stripes along its side. "It's a one-year-old cutthroat trout," she decided.

"Baby salmon can't tolerate water warmer than ten degrees or they cook to death," she continued. The children ran around, squealing "*Cooked to death!*" She bagged some larvae and poured them into plastic jars with magnifying lens tops so people could see them.

The group walked farther down the creek, where the Guide showed them an egg hatchery, a ladder-like contraption with plastic bubbles strung across the creek. Salmon eggs were placed inside the bubbles to develop into fry, safe from predators. The fry could swim in and out of the hatchery until they were old enough to escape down the creek to the ocean.

"They swim backward, looking and smelling, so they can find their way back to the same creek," she told them. "Take a mental picture." Instead the Professor took out his smartphone and snapped a selfie of himself and his wife framed by the verdant forest to send to the family as a Christmas card.

Back at the park site, the barbeque volunteers were cleaning up, scraping compostable scraps from paper plates, separating recyclables from garbage. Intrigued by the Church Warden's story, the Professor approached the tour operator as he collected his charts and maps, and asked, "Is there room in your creek enhancement society for another volunteer?"

"Sure," said the operator. "Welcome to the coast's unofficial department of wild salmon. Someone has to save them, because the government isn't."

So in late fall, when the water levels in the rivers were high enough for the fish to spawn, the Professor joined his new friends on the early morning ferry each week to volunteer at the fish hatchery on a Big Island river, near the spawning grounds for chum, coho, and chinook salmon.

Wearing borrowed chest waders and rain gear, the Professor entered the river with the other volunteers, pushing against the current to pick and net the spawning salmon, the sides of the chinook stained red, trapped by an aluminum fence mounted across the river. The volunteers loaded the netted fish into tanks and transported them to the hatchery, where they separated the males and females into different tanks.

They did this rain or shine during the spawning season. The Professor sucked the chilled air into his lungs, smelled the rain-soaked forest, the sweet scent of ferns. Sometimes bear and cougar tracks marked the tops of the tanks where two ravens sat, waiting to be tossed the morts, or fish that died in the tanks. For the first time he felt he was an islander.

Each week the group dumped about 100 test fish from the tanks into red plastic pails and weighed them. When the females felt ripe, the volunteers netted them and bonked them on the head with small clubs like police batons.

"Yes, we kill them," the Professor admitted to his astonished wife as they sipped their bedtime chamomile tea when he returned home on the evening ferry. She had a hard time imagining him dispatching any living creature. "Both the males and females are going to die anyway after they spawn. I wish there were a more humane way to do it."

He told her how they hung the salmon by the tail hooked to a rack at the hatchery to bleed. "The volunteers split the females up the tummy with their knives and squeeze the eggs into plastic pails below," he said. "Then they mix them with the milt or sperm from the males. The eggs are fertilized in ninety seconds. Then volunteers wash the eggs and place them into incubators."

"It sounds barbaric," said the wife, horrified, getting up from her chair to refill their cups from the teapot. She liked the fact that his new hobby got him out of the house each week, but this? Why couldn't he take up photography?

The Professor assured her that the dead fish carcasses were taken to other streams to fertilize their banks and add nutrients to the forest floor in the hopes that the smell would encourage chum and coho to return to them. "We think salmon can smell their home creek 100 kilometres away," he told her. "You will like this part better."

She handed him a slice of gluten-free lemon cake along with his refilled teacup.

"Over the winter months, the eggs hatch into tiny fry," he continued. "At the ponding stage, the tiny fry leave the incubator and swim into the larger tanks. When they do this, for the first and only time in their lives, they swim to the surface for air to fill their swim bladders," he marvelled. "Then they disappear underwater where they will spend the rest of their lives."

"Why do they do that?" asked his wife, returning to her

armchair and picking up her knitting, intrigued in spite of herself.

"I don't really know," confessed the Professor. "It's a new world for me. I'm learning things I never knew about."

He told her that the fry in the tanks were fed by the volunteers. "I take a pinch of fish food between my fingers and thumb, sprinkling it over the top of the tank water, and watch the fry swim up to feed, careful to keep out of sight. The fry are afraid of shadows, precursors of future predators," he said.

"When the fry are old enough, the volunteers flush them from the tanks into a nearby creek that flows into the river, where their parents come to spawn. The young salmon find their way downstream through the fresh water of the river to the salt water of the sea.

"Some eggs are taken to different streams and some are given to schools. The volunteers measure fish food in Ziploc bags to send with the fry to the schools, whose fences are decorated with wooden fish to mark their participation in the conservation project."

All this he told his wife. He had never talked so much in their married life.

"Why do you like doing this?" she asked, curious.

"Well, I'm outdoors in all sorts of weather, and I meet all sorts of people," her husband replied thoughtfully. "Some are young, some retired. Former teachers and executives. Some are fishermen, others have never fished at all. And I like to listen to the stories over coffee."

He told her about the ravens that learned to switch on the lights of a northern airport's motion sensor to warm their butts. "The volunteers call me Timmy because I bring Tim Horton Timbits to coffee sessions," he confided. "And some bring homemade tarts and cookies."

Well, he had never had a nickname before, thought his wife as she took the teacups to the kitchen. And he did like cookies, she noted. Still, it seemed a strange way to spend his time, given his bookish interests.

The next autumn, the Professor walked over to the salmon creek at dusk one evening to check if the salmon were returning to spawn. A few stars sparkled faintly in the pale sky. Pushing his way through the ferns and salal bushes, he scrambled down the bank near the confluence of the creek and the harbour.

He watched for a swirl in the water, the slap of a fish tail, a shadow moving underwater over stones on the stream bed. Signs of the salmon.

We don't really know where they have been, he mused. A young salmon can swim thousands of nautical miles, to Alaska and beyond, or to the middle of the Pacific Ocean. With a brain the size of an almond it can memorize the position of the moon, the stars, the sun, the tides and the currents, the smell of fresh water in its home creek, even metals in the soil of the stream bank, so it can find its way home to recreate and die.

Only one per cent will make it. Ninety-nine per cent will

be eaten by seals, bears, birds, and other fish—in fact, coho like baby chum. Or they will be killed by warm water temperatures, environmental disasters, or unknown ocean events.

Maybe there is a God after all, he reflected. Call it the Great Spirit. Or the Maker, or Honyawat, the Creator. Or SaghaleeTyee, Our Father. Or NamiPiap, Elder Brother.

Since the time of Creation, a miracle of survival, life everlasting. He prayed it would continue.

DOCK DEBATES

THE MEMBER OF PARLIAMENT FOR the Salish Sea was on the ferry sailing between the Mainland and Big Island when she saw the column of black smoke spiraling over the low-lying islands hunkered down on the horizon beyond the ship's bow. A crew member tracked her down in the cafeteria where she was drinking coffee at a table with her ferry caucus, as she called her constituents, listening to their concerns and complaints.

"The government dock on the southern island is on fire," he told her.

Coastal born and bred, she replied: "Thanks. I already figured that out." She knew from experience that only old, smouldering creosote-soaked planks and pilings produced oily streaks like those now smearing the sky.

As her tablemates rushed to the ship's cafeteria windows to speculate over the source of the smoke, she reached for her government-issue Blackberry and called the Joint Rescue Coordination Centre for further information. The Rescue Centre was not technically responsible for docks but usually was on top of coastal emergencies. "Nobody hurt, no fuel tank explosions so far," the Rescue Centre official assured her. "Things seem to be under control."

The MP was en route from her Ottawa office to her home on Big Island, but she transferred to the inter-island ferry when she reached port. By the time she arrived at the south island, most of the dock fire was out. She assessed the damage, aware that she would need to find the federal funding to rebuild the island's only public dock.

The freight shed was destroyed, she noted. The wide planks of the wharf deck itself were gone, no surprise given its fuel-soaked history. Several small craft, including the baker's delivery boat, the Canadian Coast Guard Auxiliary's Zodiac, and the runabout of a caretaker from a nearby islet had been rescued and were now moored to red buoys in the harbour.

The wharf itself had been reduced to flame-blackened pilings protruding from the seabed. The metal ramp that normally led from the wharf deck to the floats below had been hauled ashore and was leaning precariously on the rocky slope below the fuel tanks, which, thank the Lord, had been spared from the flames.

To her surprise the ferry slip, which sheathed the inter-island ferry on arrivals and departures, seemed unharmed, aside from smoke damage to the metal gates and lighting infrastructure.

Several of the volunteer fire crew had retired to the pub to celebrate their success in saving the island forest from going up in flames, jeopardizing islanders and their homes, leaving a corporal's guard to hose down the smouldering embers threatening the charcoaled pilings, the remaining relics of the dock, and the charred floats below.

The MP parked her car in front of the Wharf Store and entered the pub below to congratulate the volunteer fire crew, promising them that finding the funds to rebuild the island's government dock would be her priority.

She cut her political teeth on that dock. After the election, when the votes were tallied and the victory speeches finished and tearful opponents had conceded defeat and she realized to mounting disbelief that she was really, truly the Member of Parliament for the Salish Sea, the dock presented her first challenge, the wharfinger wars.

Before the Modern Era, as she termed her own election, the last remaining patronage perk accorded to coastal MPs of the governing party was the right to choose the person who supervised the government dock, distinguished by its red handrails, the lifeline linking the small coastal communities with the outside world. In many cases they were accessible only by logging roads or had no road access at all, and were separated from their neighbours by intractable swaths of forest. And islands were marooned on the ocean.

Nearly all supplies and people, dead or alive, came or left by boat, barge, or ferry. Small float planes, usually Beavers or Cessnas, roared up to the dock and dispatched their passengers, who perched precariously on the aircraft's pontoon and lurched over open water to the relative safety of the dock, dragging their luggage with them.

The wharfinger position was much coveted since it allowed the appointee to keep a portion of the fees collected from boaters who moored their vessels at the dock, in return for monitoring rowdy boating parties and generally maintaining peace, order, and good government.

Since she was not a member of the Governing Party, this plum was not open to the newly elected MP to award. She was stuck with the wharfinger appointed by her predecessor, a gruff redneck who, alas, had failed to survive the Green wave washing over the islands in the Salish Sea. And the wharfinger was assiduous in the application of his duties.

No boat was too small to charge fees, no hour too late to collect them. And no group was exempt, including the seniors of the Old-Age Pensioners League who came over in their powerboats from neighbour islands to play softball in the island's ballpark, or the Rector who tied up to the dock while she conducted the island's church services.

The Wharf Store owner, who also owned the pub below, complained that boaters who stopped for gas or groceries were charged a toll to step ashore. When the wharfinger followed customers seeking a cool beer on a hot summer day into the dockside pub to collect fees, the incensed owner threatened to evict the wharfinger from the premises.

Beer-cooled heads prevailed to keep the peace.

The subject came up at the MP's semi-annual constituency meeting held in the Community Hall up the road from the dock. She arranged the Hall chairs in a circle, reasoning that she would be an equal among equals, to hear local issues. As soon as she took her seat, the community cat took a break from his mouse patrol in the kitchen and wound his sleek body around her ankles, purring a warm welcome.

"It's not fair," said the Wharf Store owner. "Other islands allow a two-hour grace period before collecting fees.

"If he shakes down my pub customers again, I will lay into him with a pike pole," he added. The owner was a retired boom man who spent his working life balancing precariously on the logs floating in the booming grounds, sorting them into the various flat booms that would be towed to the sawmills or pulp mills along the coast.

The MP promised to confront the wharfinger. She found him moving boxes at the community Recycling Centre, a sideline activity, gingerly picking his way through the abandoned bicycles, cartons, unidentifiable items, and other flotsam of island life.

"Why can't you allow boaters the same two-hour grace period they are permitted on the other islands?" she asked him.

"Because it's not in the Regs," he replied. "Them others are Fisheries docks. Department of Transport owns mine."

He whipped out a set of tattered, folded government regulations from the back pocket of his paint-spattered jeans and showed her, under Section X, paragraph Y, subsection W, that there was absolutely no provision for any grace period on a Transport dock. He stuck the papers back in his pocket, turned away, picked up his shovel, and resumed his work. Subject closed. Everybody knows Regs are Regs.

She sighed as she trudged down the hill toward the pub and that cooling glass of cider. She knew what she had to do.

It wasn't her only dock challenge in her far-flung coastal riding.

She saved one community's dock from closure by unearthing an obscure and ancient treaty between Canada and the US dealing with the crab fishery, arguing successfully that the dock was an international marine shipping facility that must be available to foreign fishermen who had, in fact, long abandoned the area. The busy bureaucrat who handled the file told her that he couldn't alter the closure order. "But we can drop it to the bottom of the list," he told her, adding passing time might erode the issue.

When Fisheries announced that work must be halted on a new dock on another island because the salmon fishing season was due to open, she saved the day by suggesting that construction continue until the salmon actually appeared. The salmon obligingly cooperated by showing up after the dock was completed.

She knew the devastating impact on a coastal community if the fuel dock was closed down; if the commercial fishing fleet and the sports fishermen couldn't buy gas, they bypassed the community and it dwindled away to a few empty shacks on the forest shore. No fish meant no fish in the smokehouse for Aboriginal communities that usually shared the same shoreline with more recent residents.

She knew better than to call fishermen "fishers."

She was born in a fish camp located below the steep slope of a northern inlet, where her father was manager of the cannery that perched on pilings drilled into the seabed below. She grew up with her siblings in the wooden cabin skidded ashore from an abandoned float camp, walking narrow planks slick with rain in spring and fall and snow in winter to clamber aboard the school boat that ferried the camp "rats" to school in a pulp mill town at the end of the inlet.

When the cannery closed, the family moved to town, but she never forgot where she came from, the black spruce forests with their wild witch trees, the porpoises frolicking through the frothing waves, the black fin of an orca slicing through a riptide, the swirl of a school of herring below the surface of the sea, the excited cries of the seabirds circling overhead before diving for their dinner, the drone of crew boats whipping up and down the inlet, and most of all the intoxicating smell of seaweed strewn on pebbled beaches, the salt tang of the ocean itself, the damp touch of fog on her face.

It took her a year to arrange the transfer of ownership of the southern island's dock between government departments, a year of wheedling and coaxing bureaucrats and government MPs. In the House of Commons, she used her precious opportunities in Question Period to argue that all communities should be treated equally when it came to providing space on the government dock for boaters, who were so important to the small island economies.

She hinted darkly at discrimination based on voting practices; everyone knew only three people on island voted for the Governing Party. In the end, at a cost of hundreds of thousands of taxpayer's dollars in time and legal fees, the dock was transferred from Transport to Fisheries, allowing visiting boaters the two-hour grace period for visitors enjoyed by the neighbour islands.

Angry confrontations between the wharfinger and the Wharf Store owner slowed to a simmer as boaters came ashore to devour a lamb or salmon burger with their beer on the porch of the pub. Play resumed between the teams in the inter-island OAP softball league. Island life regained its normal placid pace.

There was time for boaters to walk the kilometre up to the General Store to refresh their groceries and ice supplies— the Wharf Store specialized mainly in bait and fishing licences and some staple canned goods—with a stop for a pint in the pub before shoving off from the floats.

The wharfinger still swooped down the ramp like an

osprey after its prey when the two-hour time period for boaters was up, but the only ruffled feathers were among the black-winged cormorants that stood on guard on top of the pilings lining the ferry slip.

Until the dock burned down.

After the fire, the MP for the Salish Sea pulled out all political stops. She and her small staff wrote letters to the Fisheries Minister and made phone calls from her Ottawa office. She visited the regional Fisheries office in town, signing the book at the security entrance and sitting in grey-celled offices while bureaucrats leafed through the estimates to show her there was no money for west coast wharf replacements.

A hurricane force wind in the Maritimes had destroyed community wharves in vote-rich fishing villages, explained the Superintendent for Small Boat Harbours, and building new docks for the Atlantic lobster boats and cod-fishing fleet had siphoned off all available funds.

She went on radio talk shows, gave media interviews, enticed television crews to broadcast the plight of an island without a public dock. She explained that the few private wharves were too small to accommodate local traffic.

The fire had destroyed the dock lights. She recounted how, in the winter dark, the island school children used flashlights to navigate two planks, slippery with frost, laid across the blackened piers and down the narrow ramp to access the school boat. She described how the volunteer ambulance crew, battling ice, snow, and rain, carried the stretchers over those planks to load the sick, the dying, and the dead, guided by the marine lights of the water taxi standing by to transport them to hospital or to the funeral home on the Big Island.

She explained that the government dock served the mail boat that offloaded the newspapers and bulky bags of letters and packages that were then hauled across the burned timbers, where sea stars clung to the pilings below the surface amid skeins of seaweed swayed by the tidal currents.

Other wharf users included the commercial fishing boats, Fisheries and Canadian Coast Guard vessels, recreational boaters and tour boats, the local baker who ferried bread and pies to the neighbour islands. There were also boat fuel deliveries, the RCMP, the Royal Canadian Navy on training cruises, the water taxi, Hydro, highway and phone maintenance crews, and the district water system engineers.

Even Santa Claus, who arrived from the American islands across the watery International Boundary with his bag of goodies for the local children every dark December, tied up at the government dock.

A popular political columnist on the Mainland wrote that the government's refusal to rebuild the only public dock on island exposed Ottawa "as a useless barnacle on the nation's body politic," to the satisfaction of the Church Warden, reading his newspaper in his recliner, his tabby cat batting the pages with its paws.

But there was no response from Ottawa on the dock file.

By the second year the MP for the Salish Sea had bombarded the Fisheries offices with emails and phone calls until she won an appointment with the same regional bureaucrat, who explained that ice flows in the St. Lawrence River at breakup had torn out many small wharves in Quebec, melting any chance of replacement funds for the Pacific coast wharf.

She spoke in Parliament about how the "huge, hulking, blackened smelly ruin of a dock" had become a metaphor for alienation of coastal voters. Opposition MPs applauded, hooting and hollering in the Commons chamber in the traditional response.

She wrote again to the Fisheries Minister, who came from the Maritimes. Two months later he replied, "Unfortunately all program funding this year is fully committed to other priority projects and tendering of this project must await additional funding availability. I understand the urgency of this problem and regret that I cannot be more helpful at this time."

Her pleas brought no response. Her fellow coastal MPs didn't care. They had bigger fish to fry in their communities.

She plotted how she could accost the Prime Minister himself, if only she could approach him personally. As an Opposition member, she couldn't speak to him in the government lobby that paralleled the House of Commons chamber. That privilege was restricted to government MPs. Security guards screened visitors to the PM's corner office.

Finally her chance came, an opportunity to attend a glittering gala in the National Arts Centre, staged for some visiting Head of State. Glittering galas were considered non-partisan and all followed the same format. There were two hosts, one French Canadian, usually a pretty girl with marvelous hair and high heels, and one Anglo Canadian, usually male with short hair and a drab suit. Alternating in French and English, they greeted the audiences and introduced the performers that invariably included a children's choir, a Ukrainian Canadian dance troupe, Maritime fiddlers, a sexy, smoky-voiced Quebec singer of the LGBT (lesbian, gay, bisexual, transgender) community, Aboriginal drummers, and parka-clad northerners playing Inuit games. During intermission, the MP for the Salish Sea located the PM talking to the Fisheries Minister in the NAC lobby. Elbowing her way through the cloying lobbyists and security guards, she asked him loudly why her constituents were forced to risk life and limb in the winter storms without a government dock while money was spent on Ottawa galas and other frivolities. Some members of the media swung their cameras and microphones toward her.

The PM, a savvy political veteran who liked the coastal MP and supported more women in politics, turned to his Fisheries Minister for the answer. The Fisheries Minister, looking like a gaffed fish, said he would look into it. An aide smoothly shouldered the MP away from the political powerhouses and the crowd of interested spectators.

But she was satisfied.

In due course, another letter from the Fisheries Minister landed in the MP's in-basket in her obscure office, located on the extreme edges of the Parliamentary Precinct. He wrote that he "appreciated the importance of the damaged dock to the islanders" and he was pleased to announce that repairs had been included in the next fiscal year's expenditure plan.

In due course, a regional bureaucrat contacted the MP and advised her he had been instructed to consult with the islanders to learn their views on the plans for a new dock. The MP called a public meeting in the Community Hall to discuss the dock.

The Fisheries delegation arrived by ferry armed with plans, charts, and blueprints that were tacked up on the walls of the Hall. The community gathered around long tables, set with pencils and notepads. In the kitchen members of the Women's Club brewed urns of coffee and plated cookies. The community cat took up his position at the door to scrutinize the visitors for possible treats.

It would be a long afternoon.

The Chair of the Community Club presided. "Welcome to the Island Ad-Hoc Committee on Dock Replacement," she said, and then introduced the MP and the Superintendent of Small Boat Harbours and suggested the islanders sitting around the tables introduce themselves.

They included the usual suspects: the president of the local service club, the tourist lodge operator, the local marina operator, the island gravel truck operator, the RCMP Corporal who came by boat from the Salish Sea detachment on the neighbour island, the island ferry terminal manager, who sold tickets and advised on delayed departures and arrivals, the head of the emergency rescue volunteers, the school trustee, the Wharf Store owner, the wharfinger, the Church Warden, and other interested islanders.

The Superintendent of Small Boat Harbours was a long, lean man with an easygoing manner that sustained him through his encounters with the public during public consultations. He introduced his colleagues, most of whom were in an "acting" capacity. They wouldn't be in their present posts long enough to live with the results of their decisions, thought the MP, perched on her stool on the sidelines where she could see and hear, but not intrude on the public discussion.

The Superintendent distributed printed copies of Option One, which featured a large wood-planked wharf, similar to the one destroyed by the fire, with an aluminum ramp that dropped down to a few narrow floats that would allow passing boats to access the fuel pumps and the float plane to tie up at the end. There was little room for small boat moorage for locals or visitors.

The Ad-Hoc Committee members squinted at the drawings. "Not enough room for visiting boaters to tie up," said the wharfinger. The lodge operator, whose landlocked inn had no ocean access, agreed. "Not a problem," said the local marina operator. His floats were too far down the harbour to service lodge visitors, but he needed all the business he could attract.

"The ramp is too steep for the schoolchildren who need to access the school boat during the school year," said the school trustee, thinking of the winter tides that could vary in height as much as fifteen feet.

"Why do we need a wharf at all?" said the gravel truck operator. "Why don't we build a concrete bulkhead along the shore and fill it with gravel instead?"

No one commented on this. The Fisheries officers nervously shuffled their papers. A bulkhead? What would Treasury Board say? The design of government docks must meet TB specifications. So must railway freight cars and government signage.

The ferry terminal person peered at her copy of the drawing. "I don't know," she said. "This plan has a new ferry terminal building opening onto the government wharf. Those are different jurisdictions. Might not be allowed."

There was no comment on this either. Everyone present knew that federal Fisheries claimed the fire originated in the electrical workings of the provincially owned ferry slip. Insurance was an issue.

The Superintendent handed round Option Two, which presented a small wharf ramped down to a maze of finger floats to accommodate small powerboats and sailboats, leaving larger gin palaces to moor out in the harbour.

"Too many floats," said the local marina operator, who feared the competition provided by the government dock. "Wind and wave action during the winter storms would tear them out."

Several committee members nodded. A recent south-easter funneling through the cove had jackknifed the ramp to the Wharf Store's private dock, drowning the island's internet connection that was attached to the ramp and was deposited underwater on the seabed. This limited contact with the Mainland.

"The increased small boat traffic might interfere with the ferries," said the ferry terminal manager, peering at the plan through her rose-coloured glasses. "It is still attached to the new ferry terminal."

"It would probably be okay if streamed along the shoreline," said the wharfinger, anticipating many more moorage fees paid by both locals and visitors. The more boats, the more fees to collect and the greater his income, thought the Church Warden, although he kept silent. Island incomes were marginal at best.

"Not enough room for the police boat to tie up," said the Corporal. "Same for the Coast Guard Search and Rescue vessel," said the Emergency Services Coordinator, who also served as a Canadian Coast Guard Auxiliary volunteer.

"I suggest we look at my proposal for a gravel-filled bulkhead instead of a new wharf," said the gravel truck operator.

"If we built it deep enough and wide enough, the police and Fisheries boats could tie up."

The MP mentally reviewed the various environmental assessments that would cascade from any attempt to disturb the seabed with a gravel-filled bulkhead, but again she kept her mouth shut. This idea wasn't going anywhere.

"Well, what ideas do you all have?" challenged the Superintendent, collecting his copies of Option One and Option Two from the tables.

Well! While the Fisheries officials pinned copies of Option One and Option Two and various survey maps on the plywood walls of the Community Hall, the committee members got to work with pencils and paper, drawing their own versions of their preferred options. They created big docks and small docks, with varying configurations of attached floats, depending on their experience and economic interests.

The pub owner, who in fact did not own a boat, drew a series of floats framing a rectangular body of water, almost doubling the number of moorage spaces. The Church Warden, who did own a boat, noted acidly there was not enough space to turn a sailboat or powerboat around in the enclosed sea space, or to enter or exit the interior moorage berths.

The ferry terminal manager drew a dock with a large water lane separating the ferry slip and the proposed government dock. The gravel truck operator drew a large cement bulkhead filled with gravel.

When they were finished, they turned their proposals

over to the Superintendent. Everyone stood and stretched and poured themselves cups of coffee and helped themselves to cookies, feeding crumbs to the cat. Then they folded the tables and stacked the chairs and closed up the Hall. The Church Warden left the key in its well-known hiding place under a piece of firewood.

The MP did a little constituency business on the Hall porch on her way down to the ferry terminal, accompanied by the Fisheries officials, who chatted among themselves, relieved to have concluded another public consultation.

Time passed. The government fiscal year ended. Early in the new one, contracts were let and work on the new dock began. What emerged was a compromise. It had a dock large enough to tie up the police boat and to permit cars to drive down, discharge passengers, turn around, and leave. It had an aluminum ramp that led down to several floats, but not too many.

It did not have a cement bulkhead filled with gravel, but the dock itself was surfaced with cement. The provincially owned ferry company built a new terminal in cartoon colours on its own water lot. The terminal had doors on the dock side but they opened onto thin air. They did not actually connect to the dock itself, preserving provincial autonomy guaranteed under the Constitution Act.

The cormorants on watch on the pilings lining the ferry slip flapped their wide wings and decreed the new dock was perfect.

So did most islanders.

The MP for the Salish Sea wrote a letter thanking the Superintendent of Small Harbours, adding that she had received a few more dock repair requests from other island communities in her riding that had monitored the dock construction with great interest and greater envy.

Reading her letter in his drab grey office, the Superintendent chuckled and checked his latest estimates. There was zero money for west coast dock repairs, he wrote the MP. All available funds had been allocated to the Atlantic Provinces to finance offshore oil and gas drilling activities. He suggested it would take an earthquake-triggered tsunami to free up funds for the west coast.

The MP added his reply to her files. She would look for other opportunities to score political points for her isolated constituents.

There was always another day, another gala.

LIGHTS OUT

ON THE FIRST DAY OF fall, the hydro power went off on most of the island. "Damn," said the Professor's wife to the white cat with the chocolate ears that was grooming herself on her favourite perch, the coffee table in the living room.

The wife rarely swore, but she was not prepared when the lights went out just as she sat down with a glass of sherry and the local newspaper in the recliner chair and pressed the remote to turn on the television for the supper hour news. The TV set abruptly went dark. The silence rang in her ears. The white cat yawned, jumped down from the coffee table, and settled in her lap.

It was the fleeting moment when the autumn sun had set behind the tall trees across the channel and dusk was rapidly fading into dark, lit by sporadic flashes from the lighted marine buoy in the harbour (one flash—four seconds dark—one flash) that warned of danger underwater. Turning in her chair, she peered out the living room window. Lights shone on the neighbour island, including the blinking red light on a transmitter tower.

So this was a local problem. She brushed the cat from her lap, stood up, and went to the hall cupboard to rummage for storm lights. It was just her luck that her husband was on the Big Island volunteering at a local fish hatchery and planned on staying the night.

The couple was becoming accustomed to the power outages that plagued the island during the late fall and winter nights, darkening homes and thawing food-filled freezers, forcing the General Store staff to pull on sweaters and woollen caps to serve their customers, and the ferries to use emergency power sources when docking. There were no streetlights beyond the dock.

But it was still September, redolent with ripe blackberries and sun-warmed plums waiting to be picked and the sweet smell of newly cut hayfields. She felt ambushed by the threat of winter.

The wife reached to the top shelf of the cupboard and pulled down the emergency light from Canadian Tire. It had fluorescent tubes that lit up a room and an AM and FM radio channel and shrieked like a siren at the push of a button. It didn't turn on. She couldn't find the recharger. "Damn," she said again.

She located a blue flashlight with no batteries. She searched unsuccessfully for candles.

She found all sorts of things—wind chimes, light bulbs, a handsaw, a can of WD-40 to oil rusty hinges, but nothing that would illuminate the darkening house. Finally she unearthed a battered old camp lantern with a pale, flickering bulb that she took with her glass of sherry into the bedroom. The cat followed.

Might as well go to bed. No telling when the Hydro crews would arrive by boat and fix the problem. Both wife and cat were asleep, cuddled up under the quilts, when the fire alarm squeaked, the TV squawked, and the lights came back on sometime during the night.

She learned what happened the next day when she joined other members of the island choir on their regular visit to the housebound wife of the local sheep farmer, crowding the small house to sing mournful hymns and lively Scottish ballads and drink tea and gossip.

"That new builder was clearing some ground in the valley when his backhoe caught the power lines and pulled down the whole kit and caboodle, the lines and the hydro pole," announced the alto soprano who lived nearby. "What a mess. Instead of staying in the cab, as he is supposed to do with those live lines snaking and sparking all over the road, he jumped out and grabbed a plank and tried to clear the lines from his truck."

The invalid, her face rosy from her afternoon nap, tried to stay awake at the news. "So stupid," she said, her blue eyes blinking. "Could have been electrocuted." She nodded off again in her chair.

The singers swapped stories about the difficulties the premature power outage had caused them. "I couldn't drive my car over the downed power lines and I was forced to stay the night with a friend," recounted the alto soprano. Her friend was a bachelor. The other singers suspected she planned to do that anyway.

The bed and breakfast owner, also stranded down in the valley at a friend's place, crossed the creek in the dark and climbed the hill in her sandals to meet her guests arriving by car on the evening ferry. They were fine when they drove back to the B&B. Her place had a generator for a backup power supply.

The Professor and his wife also had a generator, a fifteen-year-old 5000 kW Tecumseh model with a pull start that was so difficult to operate that, in fact, it had never been used. The island mechanic had taken it to his shop behind the General Store, cleaned it up, and replaced the plugs. He allowed it worked pretty well.

But he suggested the couple replace it with a smaller 6500 kW Champion (a Honda "knock-off," he explained) with an electric starter that could be trickle-charged from the domestic (20 volt A) supply. "There is not much of a secondary market for fifteen-year-old pull-cord generators," he added. "Any off-island purchaser would have to come to the island to remove it."

He would be willing to take the Tecumseh off their hands in return for the work he'd put into it, he told them, wiping his hands with an oil-stained rag. Of course the Champion would need to be purchased in town and transported to the island and installed, a job that would require two men, time, and ferry costs.

The bargain was made. Each party to the deal shook hands, satisfied with the result.

These discussions, which took place over the summer months, had not yet been resolved, so the issue was academic on the first day of fall when the power went out. But at least they had a decent wood supply piled up in the yard for their wood stove and fireplace, ensuring the couple both heat and food during the darkest winter weather, when they suffered bouts of bronchitis triggered by the sooty wood smoke, making hauling firewood a chore.

The wood, however, did not come cheap. The local service club provided chunks of wood, collected from "blow-down" timber harvested from the Hydro right-of-ways, and delivered by truck to seniors and widows and the infirm, including those islanders, like the newcomers, who did not have a chainsaw to supply their own firewood.

A donation to the service club was expected in return, although this was not explicitly negotiated, depending on the circumstances. Given the couple's comfortable, pension-supported affluence compared to their neighbours' financial situation, the anticipated donation was expected to reflect the market value of the firewood.

The wood, generally cedar, aspen, and some fir, required

chopping and stacking. For this task the couple turned to the Pirates, a group of young people who had arrived in their sailboats and dropped anchor in the harbour earlier that spring.

It was not clear how many Pirates there were. One couple had a dog. Another had a baby. They lived on their boats or occasionally rented a small cabin onshore. They walked or biked everywhere since they did not have cars.

There was speculation that at least one Pirate couple had been street people in the past. When they boarded the ferry, backpacks strapped to their backs, there was agreement among the wharf pub regulars that they were going dumpster diving in town. The more skeptical drinkers pointed out that the treasures available for the taking at the Free Store at the Recycling Centre made such trips redundant.

Who knew? And more importantly, who cared? It was the general consensus that the Pirates, who charged double the minimum wage—cheap by island standards—were hard workers and willing volunteers who helped out serving and washing dishes at community dinners in return for a free meal and showers in the Community Hall.

The very afternoon the power went out the young woman known as the Pirate Queen showed up to finish chopping and stacking the wood behind the couple's cottage. She strode down the driveway, carrying her axe and wearing work boots, her long legs bare beneath a short black miniskirt.

Tattoos tortured her arms and extended to her ears. To ensure that her long dark hair did not blind her as she chopped, it was caught up in a bun.

The wife examined her doubtfully, marveling at the exquisite tattoos. "Where did you learn to chop wood?" she asked, acutely conscious that in case of an accident, a sliced foot or axe embedded in those shapely legs, medical help was not readily available.

"Ontario," the Pirate Queen replied, moving a chopping block into place. "My dad had a cabin in the north woods."

Further questioning revealed that the north woods involved the most exclusive lakefront in Central Canada and that the Pirate Queen had earned a college degree at an impressive Ontario university. Intrigued but satisfied, the wife took her a glass jar of water and left the Pirate Queen briskly swinging her axe over her shapely head and—whack—down onto the chopping block, expertly splitting a chunk of cedar.

Loss of telephone communication was another problem endured by islanders, the Professor's wife reflected as she walked home from the choral singing visit. She was not complaining, just making the point. She remembered when, during the summer, an unidentified ship, dragging its anchor in local waters, pulled up an underwater marine cable connecting the island to the Mainland.

The lunch crowd gathered at the wharf pub discussed possible culprits who had created the Phone Crisis.

"It was one of those freighters that anchor in the Sound to escape paying demurrage charges in Port," said one regular, sipping a popular ale produced in a local brewery.

"Nah. It was those Canadian Navy cadets training on that minesweeper over the holiday weekend," said another, ordering the pub special, stuffed with lamb, bacon, cheese, onions, tomatoes, mayonnaise, and a secret sauce known only to the chef, a refugee from pulp mill pollution on the Big Island.

"If our NATO airplanes with their fancy equipment can bomb civilians instead of soldiers in their missions abroad, why shouldn't our Navy sever an underwater cable clearly marked on the marine charts?"

Other pub regulars ordered more beers and blamed the "gin palaces," the local name for the huge pleasure boats that frequented the local marine park. But they did agree that the only telephone repair barge was up the coast and would take several days to transit down. They knew from past experience that the telephone repair crews didn't work on holidays and would be running behind schedule.

Islanders settled down to wait out the Phone Crisis. The telephone company sent over four cell phones that were distributed to the General Store, the Wharf Store, the volunteer lighthouse keeper who kept an eye out for boaters in distress off the reef, and the ferry terminal manager.

During the week the phone company sent over two more "loan phones," one for the medical clinic and the other for the road foreman. This information was contained in the

Phone Crisis notice posted on the door of the General Store, along with a request to let neighbours know if anyone had access to a cell phone.

But cell phones didn't work well on island, unless one climbed a hill and pointed the cell phone toward the nearest town on the Big Island. Most of the time the cell phone beeped "system busy."

A key problem was the 911 service for medical emergencies, since no health care professional actually lived on island but one came from off island to hold medical clinics on specific days between ferry arrivals and departures. Another sign on the General Store announced:

ISLANDERS: BETTER HEALTH IS
NOW AS CLOSE AS YOUR PHONE

under a program called Partnership for Better Health that offered a "health support" toll-free line between the hours of 3:00 PM and 10:45 PM on weekdays only. This service, naturally, was unavailable during the Phone Crisis.

Members of the island's emergency response crew visited every senior on island to tell them if they had a medical emergency to drag themselves out into the yard and yell loudly. This actually worked for a senior when he had his stroke. Recovering consciousness, he dragged himself outside and screamed until a neighbour heard him.

The days went by with no sign of the telephone repair

barge. The pub lunch crowd speculated it was not up the coast as earlier reported, but actually in Alaska.

Many activities, such as Friday bridge in the Community Hall, were so ingrained in island life that they went on as usual. Others operated on the island moccasin telegraph; work crews mysteriously came and went about their business. Some people sent notes to the General Store asking the clerk to send milk and eggs, charged to their store accounts, back with their neighbours when they picked up their mail.

The store clerk told the pub lunch crowd that she heard the repair barge was up the coast, but the captain was in Alaska.

Finally the pub lunch crowd reported that the barge crew had turned up at the pub for lunch. Eight days after the phones went dead the phone lines hummed again.

Autumn, with its scents of lavender and freshly harvested basil, gave way to the nostril-pinching chill of winter. Dawn came later each day. When the wife opened the thermal bedroom drapes each morning she noticed that the orange mooring buoys, rescued from the chilly waters of the cove and iced with frost, glowed like candlelit pumpkins on the neighbour's dock. The tide swilled like slush ice on the calm sea.

One winter afternoon, the Professor and his wife attended a Celtic concert in the little church, featuring a young woman harpist who had driven off the icy ferry deck with her Irish harp wrapped in an old flannel blanket in the trunk of her worn car. It had snowed, and some church members came on their cross-country skis to attend the service. Outside the church the air was sharp with the smell of frozen cedar branches that snapped from the cold. The snow fell softly from the darkening sky. Inside, the altar candles cast a golden glow on the cedar walls and glinted on the strings of the Celtic harp, caressed by the young musician as she plucked her mournful plaints.

She was going blind, but only the Rector knew that. She had offered the musician a chance to visit the island and play while she still had the sight to drive.

The congregation stood to sing the twelfth-century hymn "O Come O Come Emmanuel":

Rejoice! Rejoice! Emmanuel
Shall come to thee, O Israel

when suddenly the transformer on the hydro pole on the road beside the church blew out with a loud bang, illuminating the dark afternoon with a cascading shower of blue sparks.

The church door flew open as the road foreman, dressed in his yellow emergency gear, shouted, "Everybody out! The power lines are down. Drive carefully!"

Everybody ran for the exit, offering rides to others who lived near them. The musician hurriedly wrapped her harp in the flannel blanket and followed them to find her car. The cross-country skiers stepped into their ski harnesses, put on their gloves and pushed off down the snow-filled gullies, away from the power lines on the road.

The Professor and his wife collected the harpist and the Rector, whose powerboat was moored at the dock, and took them back to their house. They sat by the open fire in the fireplace and drank whisky-laced hot toddies and listened while the harpist unwrapped her instrument and played an impromptu concert and confessed her fear that her impending blindness would deprive her of her ability to read and play her music.

The Rector silently prayed it would not, and sipped on her whisky. The visitors stayed the night, bedding down on spare cots stored in every island house for such emergencies. The snow turned to rain overnight and the Hydro crews arrived by boat before dawn to restore the power.

In the grey morning, after a breakfast of strong coffee and French toast with bacon, the Rector boarded her boat, switched on the engine and pushed off from the dock, setting course for her home island. The musician drove onto the morning ferry, her harp on the car seat beside her, and headed for the Mainland.

She never returned to the island. But the Celtic harp concert in the candlelit church became a cherished island story, embellished with each retelling until people who never set foot in the church believed in their hearts they had been there, in the pews, when the power generator blew.

Such is the power of an island memory.

BOOK THIEF

THE WOMAN WHO STOLE HER book was in church on Sunday, sitting in the second pew. The Church Warden's wife couldn't believe her eyes. There sat the thief, smiling like a saint and singing the hymns in a soulful soprano voice, acting as if she hadn't picked up the book in the ferry washroom earlier that week.

The wife had made her customary washroom visit on the ferry, following the Queen's example of never missing a loo stop because one never knew when the next opportunity arose. The wife had placed her book, carefully camouflaged under a copy of the local paper, on the washbasin countertop. The only other person in the washroom was the singer, drying her hands on a paper towel. They exchanged pleasantries and the wife closed the toilet stall door.

When she came out a minute later the newspaper was still there, but the book wasn't. Mystified, she checked under the counter and in the toilet stall. She examined the waste disposal bin. It took her a few minutes to grasp the fact that the book had vanished.

She was certain that no one else had visited the washroom in the minute or so she had been using the facilities. She washed and dried her hands at the washroom counter. She didn't know what to do.

The book, *Dropped Threads: What We Aren't Told*, was an anthology of women's stories edited by Carol Shields and Marjorie Anderson. The wife bought it at the island library's annual book sale.

She took comfort in the stories about the imaginary women who turn the routine into the exceptional, or that buttressed her own beliefs. Margaret Atwood's essay, "If You Can't Say Something Nice, Don't Say Anything At All," confirmed her own grandmother's edict, strictly adhered to by her granddaughter.

She enjoyed the stories of female friendships, marital tribulations, and sexual misbehaviour so foreign to her own experience as a virginal bride and faithful wife. Not that she had much opportunity otherwise, she thought as she turned the pages, thinking of the astonishing number of illicit relationships that threaded the fabric of island life, despite the sparse population.

The weekly line-dancing sessions in the Community Hall should create new numbers called "Swing Your Partners Round and Round" or maybe "Catch and Release."

She smiled, surprised at her own rare attempt to create a joke.

She had looked forward to finishing the final chapters. And now she might not be able to, unless she could find the book.

She went down the narrow stairs to the ferry deck. Starting at the bow, she made her way between the packed cars until she came to the Toyota Corolla, covered in island dust, where the singer sat in the front seat, smiling. The wife smiled back. There was no sign of any book.

What should she do? Rap on the window of the Toyota and say, "Did you see my book on the washroom counter?" or "Did you by any chance pick up my book by mistake?" or "When you have finished with my book I would like it back, please."

In the end she did nothing. Frustrated, she walked from the ferry to the terminal bus stop empty-handed.

Now, in church, sitting in her customary pew, she took another peek at the suspected book thief across the aisle with its worn red carpet. Looking like an angel. Another example of the deceits and deceptions that underlay so much of island life.

Like the Thong Man, she thought as the priest droned on. He appeared to be the perfect example of an impeccably dressed antique dealer who came on weekends to catalogue his acquisitions. But when he died and the movers took his personal belongings to the Recycling Centre, they contained dozens of plastic bins of men's thong underwear. Hundreds of thongs! Apparently he only used them once and then threw them away. Where? Who knew?

And the mechanic who swore he never touched a drop, until the Caterpillar operator dug his shovel into the sawdust heap in the backyard and uncovered a pit filled with hundreds of empty rye whisky bottles, to the astonishment of the clerk who stocked the liquor shelves in the General Store and knew what every islander drank and how much.

"Oh, he never drinks red wine," he would counsel a prospective dinner guest wondering what to buy his host. "He only drinks beer." Or maybe: "She likes the Pinot Grigio, not the Chardonnay."

Even the island stories belied belief, like the story of the Blue Ghost. Long ago, according to the story in the library book shelves, in the hippie era, a young woman walked off the ferry in her blue denim jacket and long skirt with her backpack and a small kettle hanging from her belt.

She asked the terminal operator about the fishboat that had drifted in to shore with three men, all dead, possibly from carbon monoxide. The fourth man, her husband, was missing, she said. When the terminal operator assured her the missing man had not turned up, the woman walked over to the Point to wait for him, saying that her husband would come for her.

There was a big storm, and some islanders out on the water saw a brightly lit fishboat racing the waves, headed for shore. They saw the woman in blue denim standing on the Point. When the boat came near, she plunged into the sea and vanished. The boat turned away, the lights went out, and it vanished too.

The island view was that when the young woman realized her husband wasn't on board she plunged into the water and drowned. Now, when there is a full moon, the blue denim ghost can be seen walking in the woods at the Point, and when a northwest storm blows a ghost ship races along the shore.

With a start, the wife heard the priest give the final Blessing and she turned her mind to nettle tea and cookies served after the service in the church basement.

She was still distressed by the book thief incident and her inability to resolve it when she took her next ferry trip to town. She sat in the hard, plastic chair in the sparsely populated ferry passenger lounge, pulling her green polyester sweater ordered from the Sears catalogue over her shoulders, probing the self-inflicted wounds to her self-image. Her depression deepened. At the time of her life when she should be most content, most satisfied with her state of being, she found herself assailed by doubt about who she really was.

The alarms of anxiety she experienced were not the normal angst about the Meaning of Life and the futility of it all, the fear of time running out, of death, common to many seniors. She had a shrewd sense of her limitations, including a sturdy but not brilliant intellect, and a conventional view of the world and her place in it.

She was neither beautiful, talented, nor so obnoxious people were forced to acknowledge her. She meekly accepted the curt indifference of the hardware clerks when she tried to explain what tool she was seeking, the snickers of the sleek young things in the retail stores when she asked for a plus size.

She believed herself to be a subservient wife to a self-absorbed husband and a dutiful mother to a distant daughter so unlike her in personality and lifestyle she sometimes wondered how she had borne her, as she hand-lettered birthday greetings and Christmas cards, scratching out Happy Holiday messages and inserting Merry Christmas and a cherub in the card series from the Heart and Stroke Association.

She believed all people were basically good, given the chance to improve themselves, their occasional bad deeds notwithstanding. She did more than her share of volunteer work and gave more than she could afford to charities. In essence, her essence, she was a good person.

This point of view allowed her to smooth over the inconsistencies of her faith, such as the loving God who ordered Abraham to slay his son, a scene depicted in a colouring book on the Bible that was so horrific she never gave it to her young godchild.

She stared out of the ferry window as the ship rounded

the Point, and she thought of the Blue Ghost and her futile search for her missing partner. Looking for each other? thought the Church Warden's wife. Who would believe that?

At least I know where mine is, she reflected. Sitting in his recliner chair with his crossword puzzle and his tabby cat.

She was aware that as she entered her senior years she had become invisible, devoid of any personality or redeeming character in the society around her. She read somewhere that women in their sixties were considered the most useless segments of the population, beyond childbearing and sexual adventures, unlikely to attract either notoriety or celebrity before they simply disappeared from view.

Born of a Catholic father and an Anglican mother, she was also aware that she suffered her share of Catholic guilt from her convent school days, but her disquiet lay deeper. It was a form of self-doubt unlike anything she had experienced since the torment of her teenage years, although the tortured exploration of who she might become now centred on who she had become. She had a sense of her Self unraveling, of dissipating like soda-water bubbles.

She realized that people might not perceive her as she did herself. Was her natural reserve, even shyness with people, viewed as arrogance and a sense of superiority among her peers? Her rare enthusiasms about certain subjects, such as bridge and babies, for example, gave a sparkle of confidence, of self-worth to her life.

But were they viewed by others as the dogmatic and dated views of approaching senility, to be indulged and ignored? If so, where was the deception, and who was the deceived?

She could see the timbered outline of an island in the channel ahead of the ferry, and thought of the silent deceptions people practised, the things people never talked about at all but were right there, in front of them, in plain sight.

On the island was the abandoned hulk of a residential school, a system set up in the last century to provide Aboriginal children with teachers and schooling where none existed, but now universally reviled as a repressive system accused of sexually and physically abusing thousands of Aboriginal students.

Her father's cousin, an Oblate priest, had taught young Aboriginal students in that school, she remembered as the island loomed out of the Salish Sea. The youngest son in a family of nine, and his mother's last chance to honour her pledge to devote one of her sons to the Church, he left his sweetheart and family in an eastern province to take up a teaching position in the isolated school.

The federal government, which had constitutional responsibility for Indians—as Aboriginal citizens were called—did not have the money or personnel to provide education to their Aboriginal charges, scattered in reserves in small coastal communities, and turned to the Church.

The young priests and nuns who were assigned to the residential schools believed they were following Holy Orders, committed to bringing education to a neglected population, people beyond reach of civil society at the time, the Oblate priest told his young cousins at a family dinner.

"We were given no Aboriginal history, no instruction in Native cultures," he told the fascinated children, brought up on stories of Cowboys and Indians. He described how, on Saturday nights, he lay in his cot in a room behind the school's chapel, listening to the young Aboriginal men drinking and dancing around the bonfires on the beach, fearful that he was going to be scalped.

While there were many reports of government agents and police bringing children to the school, the Oblate recounted how some Aboriginal parents brought their children to the school willingly, asking that they be taught reading, writing, and arithmetic so that they could do business with the traders who supplied the reserves with basic supplies, like flour, sugar, and tea.

She remembered a nun telling them at a dinner in Oblate House, "We had forty cents a day to feed, clothe, house, educate, and provide medical services for each child. People now complain the students were forced to wash dishes and scrub the floors. With such limited budgets, we all scrubbed the floors." She added bitterly, "It was part of the culture of service."

The wife reflected on how she and her classmates earned

trading cards of the Saints by scrubbing the stone steps of their modestly affluent convent school.

The nun and priests at the Oblate dinner had never been accused of any form of abuse, and certainly did not condone it, yet as a result of the actions of others, they believed that their whole lives had been in vain and submitted themselves to society's general condemnation.

The Church Warden's wife wondered why few, if any, former students came forward to say that the education they received from their residential school teachers had helped them get jobs, enter professions, leave the reserves. When the Oblate cousin died, many of his former Aboriginal students attended his funeral and told, with tears and laughter, stories of his mentorship. Where were their stories recorded?

Now, as the ferry switched course and the island with its abandoned residential school receded in the ship's wake, she wondered why she too stayed silent, why she never told her family and friends the story of her Oblate cousin, and she felt an inexplicable sense of shame.

When the bus from the ferry terminal reached downtown the wife walked over to her favourite teashop to meet her friend and recounted, with indignation, the tale of the stolen book. Her friend was a librarian, well schooled in the value of beloved books. She was sympathetic to the wife's dilemma but took a pragmatic approach.

"Maybe she didn't mean to steal the book," said the

friend, sipping her decaf Earl Grey blend. "Maybe she thought you had abandoned it and the paper."

"Not likely," replied the wife. "How many people abandon books in the loo when there are all those recycling bins on board?"

The friend persisted: "Have you ever picked up anything by mistake?"

The wife considered herself an honest person, incapable of the criminal act of theft. "Of course not," she said.

"What about the time we went to the grocery store and when we got home you found those one-dollar gloves in your purse. You said you would return them. Did you?"

"I picked them up by accident and stuffed them in my purse because that is where I keep my gloves," protested the wife. "I don't know why I did that. I kept the sales tag in my wallet for a year but we never went back to that store."

"Anything else?" probed the friend.

The wife wavered. "Then there was the time we bought the Aboriginal print for your son's wedding, and when he broke off the engagement I never unwrapped the print for a year or so. When I finally did, I found the store had wrapped two copies of the print, but I had only paid for one. I thought it was too late to return it, so I never did."

"And what about St. Joseph's statue?" the friend persisted. "The one you left planted upside down in your garden and never removed when you sold your house in town? Wasn't that deceptive?"

That was true, the wife remembered. She was super-stitious as well as religious, and wore a Celtic cross while fingering Anglican prayer beads. When she and her husband decided to sell their house in their mid-coast community to move to the island, she purchased a small plastic statue of St. Joseph, husband of Mary and Earthly Father of Jesus, reputed to be the patron saint of real estate transactions and guardian of convents.

She planted the statue in a pot and buried it in the ground upside down, feet pointing to Heaven, by the FOR SALE sign. When the house didn't sell, she unearthed St. Joseph from the pot from time to time to check if he was properly planted.

When the house did sell she forgot to remove the St. Joseph statue from its pottery grave. She wondered if the statue was still there.

"I thought I could creep back one evening and remove him," she told her friend. "On second thought, maybe not! If the door opened and the new owners appeared, could I just say 'Sorry, folks, but I left something important,' then pick up the pot and leave?"

"Well?" said the friend in a smug tone that the wife found so irritating.

"Well," the wife answered, chastened. Maybe she wasn't as nice a person as she thought. Maybe nobody was what he or she appeared to be.

The wife went back to the island on the afternoon ferry.

But God is in Her Heavens. At the library's next book sale, the wife found the copy of *Dropped Threads*. It was in fine condition.

She hoped whomever took the book had learned something she needed from it. As she had.

HARBOUR GIRL

SHE WAS A HARBOUR GIRL, with her blond-streaked hair, Siberian Midnight fingernail polish, and brown eyes spiked with mascara, like sea anemones. She wore too-tight jeans, a black leather jacket, and boots cut cowboy-style. She looked like many other girls her age in the Harbour, although she was pushing it, with her thirtieth birthday in her sights.

She escaped from her south island home by being kicked out of high school for supplying her classmates with home-grown pot, an island specialty. Shipped off to the Harbour and her aunt and uncle by her Puritan parents, she married young and spawned early, producing twin boys ten months after her teenage marriage vows, disproving rumours of premarital pregnancy, a common motivation for Harbour marriages. She was what she was, which was like everyone else in her peer group.

Her one distinguishing aspect was early widowhood when her young husband, a faller, bailed over the stern of his crew boat into the black water one night to fix his engine and never came up again.

Alcohol was involved in the marine accident. "Why are we killing our young people?" despaired the local Lutheran minister at the memorial service in the Community Hall, the young man's body laid out in the open casket, beautiful in his youth. The minister recounted horrific auto accidents, fights, shotgun accidents in the surrounding forest, and acts of alcohol-fuelled violence that had killed the Harbour's young people. Drugs and alcohol were the Pied Pipers of coastal communities, although rarely in the logging camps or on the fishing grounds themselves.

The young widow and her boys lived in the rooms over the ramshackle waterfront store her aunt and uncle owned near the entrance to the Harbour by the new fish plant. The store was painted sky blue and the black roof lured the waterborne clientele with signs advertising BEER BAIT ICE FUEL, the basic requirements of the maritime community. Feral cats roamed the dock, hoping for bait scraps.

The Harbour girl worked behind the store counter with its shelves of candy bars and mints, cigarettes and cigarette papers, packets of tobacco, and cans of Copenhagen chewing tobacco plugs for the nicotine addicts who worked in the woods and couldn't smoke on the job. She flirted with the weekend sailors who tied their powerboats, sometimes called gin palaces by the locals, up to the dock. On weekdays she served coffee to the locals who gathered each day around the communal table to pass on gossip and trade stories flavoured with a vocabulary unique to the Harbour.

"He is one log short of a load," someone might say about a colleague deemed slow on the uptake. Or "I hung a beating on him with my pike pole," referring to the pole the boom men used to sort the logs in the booming grounds. Infidelity and domestic discord were common themes: "I heard she beat him up with a vacuum cleaner."

After coffee and gossip they climbed into their pickup trucks parked outside the store, or boarded their boats tied up to the ancient dock, and dispersed to various coves and bays that collectively made up the Harbour.

Actually, there was no town known as the Harbour, which was shown on the marine charts as a narrow inlet punched through the coastal mountain range. A chain of islands guarded the entrance. The residents lived in various isolated settlements scattered around the shoreline, recently connected by a narrow road but traditionally accessed by boats, nine-horse outboard motors hung over the transoms like leeches and oil-stained life jackets stowed under the bow.

The younger ones drank beer on the government wharf, with no fear of police harassment since the local RCMP detachment was back at the ferry terminal in town to clock the speeders on the coast highway. One youth bet that he could run his outboard across the water faster than another could drive his old beater on the road circling the Harbour. The driver lost the bet.

As the older fishermen died off, their skills died with them: how to read the water for wind and rain and changing tides and currents; how to sink a prawn trap thirty-five or fifty fathoms deep to the ocean floor where the prawns lived. Maybe they grazed on krill. Nobody knew.

Few of their kids were fishermen or would experience the beauty of a mackerel sky, orcas slapping black and white tails on the sea, bald-headed eagles and wide-winged ospreys circling the cedar and Douglas fir forests on the distant mountains.

Her new man was a prawn fisherman whom she met in the Legion pub. He had curly blond hair and a body hardened by physical labour in all kinds of weather. He had KISS tattooed on the knuckles of his left hand and ASS inked on the right-hand knuckles. She read them upside down, his hands clenched around his cold, glass beer mug.

She left a note for Aunty to look after her boys and ran off to the Big Island with him, away from his angry wife, until things cooled down and the wife moved to town and they returned to the Harbour and the tidal tugs of life.

The Harbour girl liked to go out on the prawn boat, using landmarks and depth sounders to search for the red scotch buoys that marked a line of sunken prawn traps strung out over one or two kilometres of ocean bottom. She liked picking the prawn traps off the line as they were winched over the stern of the boat, filled with live, vigorously snapping prawns sparkling with water, throwing out the odd red rock lobster and shaking the pale prawns into the ice-filled coolers, baiting the empty traps with pet food and stacking them on the slippery deck ready for the next setting.

Hard enough work for a man, let alone a young woman.

She liked the song of the wind, the smell of oil and rust, the flopping sound of prawns squirming in the traps, the angry exchanges when the prawn fishermen leaned out of their cockpits shaking their fists at a competitor who laid his prawn traps over another fisherman's trap line on the ocean floor.

Not for her the wifely task of picking salal up the mountain when money was short, leaving the bundled leaves on the end of a logboom for their husbands to collect when they came in from fishing. Harbour wives were expected to stay in their kitchens close to the VHF radios when their men were on the fishing grounds to monitor the oblique messages, often silenced by radio static. A fisherman never wanted to give away too much when the boat crews asked each other how they were doing.

She liked to dump the fresh prawns, tails and all, into the salted water, cooking them for four minutes until they turned pink and then plopping them onto newspapers covering the galley table, eating them hot and greasy and flavoured with garlic butter, washing them down with a can of Coke or maybe beer.

On the way back to their dock they might check out their crab traps. Sometimes they landed a salmon that they froze for her family on their island four ferries away. She and her man rarely ate fish. Many fishermen prefer steak.

Uncle was never much of a drinker until he and Aunty took over the store, with its Mom and Pop liquor store licence, issued to small coastal communities that lacked a government liquor store. Uncle drank most of the profits in the form of bottles of Alberta Vodka, which he swilled from morning to night, tottering unsteadily down the wharf ramp, bottle in hand, to gas up a customer from the decrepit fuel dock.

The trouble started the day he was too hung over to unlock the gas pumps and snored away the morning in his bed, and the Harbour girl left the safety of the store and went down to work the fuel dock.

It was a fresh morning, the arbutus trees on the shoreline glowing ruby red in the early sun. A seagull trailed a white wake on the green sea as it took off through the narrow pass where signs posted onshore warned boaters entering the Harbour SLOW TO FIVE KNOTS, so the wash from their boats wouldn't swamp others moored at the docks nearby.

She watched as a sleek Sunray powerboat glided up to the dock and the young man at the wheel cut the engine. A real gin palace, this one, she thought.

"Gas or diesel?" she called as she caught the bow line thrown her by the skipper, who then jumped onto the splintered dock with the stern line in his hand, looping it swiftly around the stanchion with a clove hitch secured by a half hitch. He knew what he was doing, she thought. Then he checked her bow line, which annoyed her.

"Diesel," he answered. "Is the store open? I need ice."

Naturally, she thought, they all do, with their beer and wine-filled coolers and veggie stick snacks. She noticed a hooded barbeque positioned on the afterdeck of the power-boat. Sports fishing gear and nets were stashed in the locker behind the Naugahyde seats. "Yup," she answered. "We got fresh bait too."

When he nodded his consent, she fished some herring bait out of the tank attached to the dock while he walked up the aluminum ramp to the store where Aunty guarded the cash register. By the time he came back she had finished both fuelling and transferring the bait to the boat.

Stepping back, she looked the Sunray over expertly and thought of her man's prawn boat, with its high, handsome Hourston hull. A working boat, with clean but smelly fish tanks and a Coleman stove for the tea and the chowder he prepared below deck. Before she could guard her tongue she called, "Nice boat."

He was already on board, reaching for the key to turn on the ignition, but at her comment he paused and looked her over, standing on the dock in her short shorts and T-shirt and sneakers and sun-streaked hair. "Want to take a spin?" he asked.

She looked him over, in turn. Tall, tanned, cut-off jeans, wearing a hoodie as protection against the wind out on the water. A real Dude, in the lexicon of the Legion crowd. She thought of her store chores, her boys at school, her man out in the channel checking his prawn traps, her uncle snoring in his bed. Every day like every other day in the Harbour during the prawn season.

"Sure," she said, helping him release the lines and cast off, and hopping aboard the craft like she owned it.

Well! What a day that was! The Dude eased the boat past the islets guarding the Harbour and headed around the Cape, pushing the throttle forward until the Sunray was riding on the step, like the boats in *Pacific Yachting* magazine. They ran up the broad channel that paralleled the Harbour, past the deserted fish farms, whose operators had moved north in search of colder waters, the odd shuttered cottage beyond the end of road, slipping around the car ferry that waddled across the channel to the next headland, the forest shoreline flitting by, the morning sun on their backs.

She opened a beer from the cooler and crossed one bare leg over the other as she lounged back in the Naugahyde seat, watching the Dude, legs braced, guide the Sunray through the channel markers. They stopped for lunch at the Lodge, fabled haunt of old movie stars and once-famous singers, where she sat in the sun on the patio looking for all the world like a Dude herself, with her dark sunglasses and her hair with its golden streaks tied back off her face.

Then they roared on to an empty cove that formed a natural swimming pool, the water warmed by the sun-seared rocks and where mussels and barnacles glimmered under the surface of the translucent sea. They stripped off their clothes and swam until they were salt-soaked and drunk with the glory of the day.

With the setting sun on their faces, the Dude boat headed back to the Harbour and the store dock, and the girl jumped ashore. "See you around," she said, releasing her hair from its restraints.

"I guess," said the Dude, waving and gunning his boat away from dock.

A local barge operator hauling freight to the channel's small logging camps spotted the Harbour girl aboard the Dude boat and reported back to the Legion crowd when he returned to the government dock in the Harbour.

That night the Legion crowd talked of little else but the young widow and her Dude boyfriend, speculating and discussing possibilities and probabilities as they talked about how many Mainland cars had gotten off the ferry that day.

Did they make love on the warm sand beaches, cushioned with golden kelp that girdled the rocky shores? That's what the Harbour asked when people heard of the Harbour girl's uppity exploits. But who would know, except the black bear nosing the oyster shells on the beach and the river otter sliding down the bank on its belly? That is what left the local gossips tongue-tied.

When her prawn fisherman came back from his shift on the water, tired and sweaty from hauling his traps and dumping his catch onto the ice in the hold, and heard the talk in the Legion Hall, his hands tightened around his beer mug until the tattoos KISS and ASS couldn't be seen. That night he slept in his narrow berth on the prawn boat.

When his sister phoned his wife in town with the news, the women agreed that the Harbour girl was no better than she should be.

The next day the girl walked down to the dock and unlocked the gas pumps and watched for the Dude boat. But it never showed up. Which was strange. There weren't that many fuel docks in the Harbour. The Dude was going to need diesel if he was going to get back to town.

Whatever. She didn't care if he came or not; there were other Dude boats out there. And all those boats guzzled fuel.

FAMILY FEUD

AMONG THE HARBOUR PIONEER FAMILIES, two sisters married two brothers. Each couple built a home on the point of land separating two coves in the heart of the Harbour. One house looked east and one looked west.

There was no road to the point. The families travelled to work and to the waterfront store by boat for fuel and supplies, using a common dock, or they climbed the hill behind the point to the coastal highway where they parked their second-hand pickup trucks in the bush above their homes.

The union of siblings between different families was not uncommon in the Harbour. Everyone was related to everyone else in some way that was familiar to the residents, but confusing to outsiders who tried to unravel the tangle of aunts and uncles and cousins and grandchildren attending communal dinners in the Community Hall on Robbie Burns Night and other festive occasions.

Many third- and fourth-generation residents were descendants of the First Nations band that originally settled in the Harbour, intermarrying with the Portuguese and Hawaiian and English longshoremen and seamen who drifted north during the nineteenth century from Mainland ports in search of land and wives. The Finns and the Norwegians settled on the islands and inlets farther north.

But unlike some coastal settlements, where the Aboriginal and non-Aboriginal communities existed side by side in separate communities, the Harbour settlers and their Aboriginal relatives jumbled their houses together. Some never bothered to claim their Aboriginal heritage unless fishing rights were involved.

The older brother was a fisherman and the younger one worked on the log booms as a scaler, measuring the amount of timber in a flat raft of logs. He employed his skills to divide their home sites when the brothers paced the property, using a tall cedar tree as a known marker. This traditional method was later blamed for the ensuing family feud.

The cove with deeper water, suitable for a dock, was claimed by the fishing brother while the scaler settled for the shallower cove with a swimming beach for the children, and the homes were built.

Scaling timber is an uncertain occupation, defined by timber operations, market conditions, forest fires, and snow conditions. But fishing is even more unpredictable, depending on the seasons, amount and type of fish stocks, fisheries regulations, and salmon species that may not show up at all, hostage to some unknown, unseen disaster in the unfathomable ocean where the salmon spend most of their lives before returning to their spawning grounds in the coastal streams and rivers.

Most years, the scaler usually earned more money than his fishing sibling. In the nature of family relationships, he and his wife felt superior to their poorer relations, who lived a more precarious existence.

Her older sister augmented the family's fishing income by picking salal year-round, except in the spring when the new growth is too fragile, sending boxes of the greenery out on the daily coach to the buyer on the coast or the florists in town. She kept her cash earnings in the drawer in the kitchen counter near the door for easy access when she went to the waterfront store for beer and groceries.

There is an art to picking salal. The shiny green leaves must be the right colour, the right size, the right shape. The best salal grows in the forests at higher altitudes. A skilled picker can make fair money on a good day, dexterously stripping the branches from the ground-hugging bushes.

The older sister loved picking. She put on her rubber boots, packed a lunch and water flask, and sliced dog food to make sandwiches for her dog. Then they set off up the mountain for a day of harvesting in the sea-scented forests and the fresh outdoors. She did this, rain or shine, throughout the harvest seasons.

Her younger sister, flush with a scaler's paycheque, went to town to have her hair permed and to purchase flowered print dresses and mock gnomes and toadstools for her garden. She was pious and righteous in her faith and attended the shingled church in the Harbour. She and her family travelled to the local casinos in a well-used motorhome. On Saturday nights they played bingo in the Community Hall, shouting out the numbers between sips of bottled beer.

When the fish were scarce, a family outing for the older brother's family was a visit to the local garbage dump up the mountain, keeping an eye out for black bears, to shoot rats and look for treasures, such as a can of paint, a lawn chair, even a dented freezer in working condition. Once they found a twenty-dollar bill in a garbage bag! They went to the scaler's house for cake on birthdays and family dinners, bringing crab cakes in season.

Once, out on the prawn boat, the Harbour girl heard her aunties (for they were, of course, related as so many Harbour families were) discuss over the radio telephone a shopping trip to town. "You should see the stuff they have on sale here," said the scaler's wife, who was already in the Mall.

"I can't come down," said the fisherman's wife, whose husband was out on the fishing grounds. "The helicopter pilot who is logging up the mountain won't feed my chickens if I go to town."

In summer, when their husbands were at work, the sisters drove the motorhome upcountry to the Cariboo goldfields, where a friend obligingly used his small Caterpillar tractor to dig out a section of a creek bed, where specks of gold glittered on the sandy bottom under the swirling waters.

The sisters sat in their lawn chairs in the middle of the creek, wearing their rubber boots and mosquito-netted hats, their water bottles tied to their chairs, and panned for gold under the hot sun, their dogs panting on the bank nearby. At the end of a long day, they carefully separated their gold flakes into small vials that they carried in their commodious purses.

By Harbour standards, they were a tight-knit and companionable family who shared a generosity of spirit toward one another. Until the boundary dispute between their home sites on the point.

The boundary problem was discovered when the fisherman, fed up with an annual income from the wild salmon fishery that barely covered his fuel and net repairs, explored the possibility of establishing a small fish farm in the deep water off the point.

Fish farming was discouraged by many commercial fishermen who insisted the farmed fish, which sporadically escaped the underwater nets, infested the wild salmon stock with sea lice. But fish farms were tolerated by some communities desperate for jobs to offset those lost in the declining wild fisheries.

When the fisherman researched the property boundaries originally registered by his brother he found that the property line ran right through his own living room. Right down the linoleum floor between his reclining chair and the television set. The difference between the legal boundary and the established one was twenty-five feet of waterfront property.

"Your brother is a log scaler," said his wife bitterly. "He knows what twenty-five feet of waterfront is worth in the Harbour. He knew what he was doing when he registered the properties." She slammed the pots on her stove in her kitchen and stomped into her living room, now apparently on her in-law's property.

The brothers talked and walked, measuring off the paces from the landmark cedar tree. They consulted the lawyers in town. The surveyors came with their survey instruments and restaked the properties. The line still ran through the fisherman's living room. Easements and money were discussed. But nothing was resolved. Plans for the fish farm were shelved.

The sisters had their own issues. When their Granny died, they inherited a small cedar box filled with trinkets and jewellery she had collected over her lifetime. Granny was somewhat of a wild card in her youth, running off to sea with a sailor after she graduated from nursing school in town.

She signed on as a nurse on one of the fabled Empress steamships that sailed between the Mainland and China and enjoyed, according to reports that filtered back to her relatives, a life of high adventure before returning to the Harbour and settling down with a towboat captain.

According to one family fable, she acquired a beautiful

ruby ring under mysterious circumstances in Singapore. She never denied the story, smiling in silence, but she never wore the ring, which took on mythical proportions. Worth thousands of dollars, according to the fable. Given to her by her lover, a Malaysian prince!

Granny smiled and continued embroidering an altar cloth for the local church. So when the sisters emptied the cedar box of jewellery she bequeathed them, they pawed through the trinkets looking for the ruby ring.

They found, in fact, two ruby-coloured rings. One was a magnificently cut jewel, flashing fires of flame in the sunlight, cradled in an expertly crafted gold setting. The second was a dull red stone, set in a plain gold ring. No sparkle, no flame-like facets.

The older sister, by family custom, had first choice. She picked the fiery red stone and wore it joyously on her finger to every social event. The younger sister hid the plain red ring in her jewellery box and never wore it at all.

The time came when the oldest sister, mindful of the passing years and estate plans of her own, took her ring to the famous jewellery store in town, the one with the big clock on the street corner, and asked to have the ring appraised.

The jeweller pulled out his loupe and examined the ring. He looked at it this way and that way and every which way, turning it under the bright light.

"So what is it worth?" the oldest sister asked hopefully, visions of sugar plums dancing in her mind.

"Nothing," said the jeweller, removing the loupe. "At least the stone is without value. It is made of glass. The setting is worth about one hundred dollars."

The sister was stunned! She couldn't believe it! Her sacred treasure all those years! The ways she showed it off around the Harbour! She could never tell her younger sister, who might possess the real ruby, after all.

But in the way of the Harbour, the younger sister found out. She never said a word to her elder sister. She took to wearing her ruby ring, discreetly, on family occasions. She never had it appraised. She would trust in Granny.

Now, after the property feud, the sisters stopped speaking to each other. This was hard to do when they lived side by side, hanging the laundry out to dry, working in their gardens. Only the scaler's hound dog visited back and forth between the two families, spending his nights with one and his days with the other, happily feeding at both.

Years passed in this fashion.

The fisherman took his brother to court to regain the twenty-five feet of waterfront and his living room space. He lost. He took the case to a higher court. He lost again. The scaler held all the cards.

But he didn't own the dock shared by the two brothers. The scaler had to cross the fisherman's property to get to his crew boat. NO TRESPASSING signs were posted by the fisherman at the entrance to the dock. Now the fisherman held the cards.

The scaler was landlocked. The water in the cove off his own side of the point was too shallow for a dock. And he knew his brother would use his riparian rights to oppose an application for a new one.

The younger brother went to town and did his own research. He found an old, unmarked road allowance that was registered on the far side of the point from the water's edge to the coastal highway. In fact, on the edge of the scaler's property. It could provide easy road access for both families.

Maybe each brother held a winning hand. Maybe the fisherman could swap access across his property to the dock in return for access across the scaler's property to a common entry road.

Hmm.

The couples were getting on in years. The climb up the hill to the highway where they kept their vehicles was becoming steeper each passing year. The scaler's wife took matters into her own hands and decided to transfer the burden to God. She went to see her minister in the shingled church.

The minister met with each brother separately in the Legion Hall. She was a non-drinker herself, but she knew the heart of her parish was in the companionable and commodious Legion, not the Church Hall. Negotiations ensued. Each card—the road access versus dock access—was played.

The result was a draw. The right to access the dock was swapped for the right to access the road allowance and the coast highway. The scaler adjusted the property line to exclude the disputed living room from his land and return it to his brother. The costs were paid by the fisherman.

The agreements were finalized over beer and bingo in the Legion Hall. Amiable, if precarious, family relations were resumed. The sisters agreed to bequeath both ruby rings to their niece.

Then the brothers found there was a problem with the water rights to their common well that served as their households' domestic water source. Apparently the water rights had not been properly filed in some distant past by the original settler on the point. A crisis loomed.

They decided, over another beer, to leave the water rights issue for the next generation to resolve. Maybe, at some future time, the Harbour would have a municipal water system and both properties would be serviced with water piped to the property lines.

Then, maybe, there would be no more family feuds.

FAMILY WEDDING

I T WAS THE BRIDE'S IDEA to have her wedding on island. Her ties were tenuous. She was the daughter of a distant cousin in a distant place. Still, she was family, wasn't she? Her groom was from the Big Island and had visited the island as a child and had pleasant memories of sunshine and sea stars on the rocks. Besides, it was probably cheaper than holding the wedding in town.

The role of wedding host fell to the Church Warden, or more specifically his wife, the relative involved. She remembered the groom as a small child bashing abandoned crab shells and rock-bound mussels with driftwood sticks on the island's stone-littered beaches. So she agreed to her cousin's request that they host the family wedding.

The island had few amenities to support a wedding party. There was the General Store and post office, the pub down by the wharf, the seasonal lodge, a handful of homes offering bed and breakfast. The store provided half a dozen tables where the locals gathered for mid-morning coffee and cinnamon buns. The Women's Club catered funerals and birthday parties in return for a small contribution.

In summer the Community Hall showed movies on Friday nights to divert the few bored tourists who walked up from the wharf in search of island distractions. There was no public transport or taxi. Islanders shared rides with people they knew, which was pretty much everyone who lived there. Visitors could hitchhike or hoof it.

The cousin assured her relative that access to the church would not be required, to the Church Warden's disappointment. The bridal party planned to be married on the beach in the National Park, above the surf line and below the high tide mark. Dogs and wedding parties were restricted in the Park itself, the former to the leash and the latter to size, which excluded large family wedding groups.

The Queen's beach was public property, beyond bureaucratic rules and regulations, but such events took careful planning, given seasonal storms and tidal surges.

The Church Warden and his wife offered their house for the reception, and, as a wedding gift, paid for a week's rent on a beach cottage for the bridal couple. The cost to them as hosts did not seem insurmountable, she thought, mentally calculating the food required for family house guests.

More unsettling was the prospect of the family gathering

itself. The wife did not know why her family so unnerved her. While never very confident, she felt reasonably competent in the presence of her friends and neighbours and carried out her routine island tasks without undue stress.

But her family put her off balance. She felt uncertain, on edge, in some way inferior, the way she felt long ago as a gawky wallflower sitting on the benches strung along the wall in the gym at her high school dances, ignored by the sweaty-palmed boys and smug, self-assured girls, who gyrated confidently on the dance floor to the brassy music of the high school swing band.

In the presence of family members she burned the food. Her hands grew clumsy and she dropped things, forcing her to extend her back leg, bend her arthritic knee, and awkwardly swoop her arm downward to the floor, swishing her hand around until it brushed against the dropped object and her fingers could retrieve it, conscious of the half-hearted attempts by other family members to assist her.

She felt humbled by her daughter's barely concealed disdain, her curt replies to her mother's hopeful queries about her daughter's life off island. Her brother disliked her and her sister rarely thought of her. Only her niece, absorbed by the continuing reality show of her own life—her boyfriend was cheating on her again, his old girlfriend told her so at a dramatic encounter in the supermarket—had a hug, a kind word, a kiss on her aunt's Avon-creamed cheek.

Her husband dismissed them all as incompetent fools of

no importance. Just like he viewed his wife, she thought with a rare flare of resentment.

Possibly the family wedding would give her an opportunity to redeem herself, to reveal the welcoming and gracious person she secretly knew herself to be. She started making lists, checking linen, counting the cups and glasses she collected from the Free Store and her potluck supper dishes stored in the top cupboard above the fridge in her kitchen.

She remembered her own wedding back in the day, as the young people called it. A simple affair, reflecting the values of her parents who struggled through the Depression and her own status as a wartime baby, brought up on ration books and unsweetened rhubarb and dressed in her older cousins' outgrown outfits.

She had worn a white cotton piqué dress, a simple shirtwaist with a matching hair band, and carried white daisies—a public testimonial to her virginal status—purchased at Eaton's department store in town. Her groom wore new suspenders under his navy blazer and a white shirt and an unfamiliar and unflattering bow tie anchoring his bulging Adam's apple that bobbed up and down throughout the ceremony.

Their wedding was held in the small wooden church in the mid-coast logging community where they met, its altar draped with patchwork quilts stitched together by the pioneer wives, whose farmer husbands cleared their homesteads out of the forests, chopping down and burning the timber on land pre-empted from Crown land to encourage immigrants to settle on the coast.

But her wedding was not without its share of drama. The local organist was tipsy with cider and sentiment and tittered her way through the wrong hymns. Midway through the service a sudden coastal shower cut off the power in the dim little church and the nearby Canadian Legion Hall where the ladies of the Women's Auxiliary were preparing the wedding supper of grilled salmon, potato salad, and coleslaw, followed by apple and lemon meringue pie. Undaunted, they hauled out the Coleman stoves from the earthquake emergency stores stashed in the Legion kitchen to finish cooking the meal.

And to add spice to the family history, her bridesmaid—her younger sister—and the best man were found smooching in a closet in the Legion Hall when the lights went back on. Everyone was rain-drenched scurrying from the church to the Hall, creating a run on supplies of rye whisky and homemade wine to warm the wedding party.

Years later, here she was, hosting the wedding of her cousin's daughter. The bride and her groom wrote their own vows and planned to conduct their own service, wearing wedding wreaths woven from native plants collected from the forest. When they applied for a licence to marry in the park and informed the Park Warden about their plans, he threatened alarming penalties if they disturbed the forest flora or littered the park with confetti. A bouquet and boutonnieres were hastily ordered from the florist shop in town.

The Church Warden, mindful of other legalities, referred the couple to the island's marriage commissioner, a tiny woman with the benign expression of one who had seen it all and enjoyed what she saw, shutting her eyes to what she didn't.

"Why did you apply for this position?" asked the Warden's wife, curious. "You must have been marrying people for a dozen years now."

"I like peeping into their lives," the commissioner said candidly. "It gives me a glimpse of how other people live. Like watching a stage show."

Most island weddings were held out of doors, although the commissioner tactfully discouraged house and garden venues after one wedding was hurriedly moved to another site when the deer ate all the flowers in the garden beds and patio pots the night before the ceremony.

"Under the authority vested in me by the Province of British Columbia, I now pronounce you man and wife," she told a beaming couple teetering on roller-skates, wearing formal clothes, at home plate in the island's baseball park.

She married a couple in the rain in the community park, under grey skies and the drenched arches of evergreen branches, where the bridal party wore raincoats with their gumboots and the bride clutched her bouquet of dripping spring flowers whose fragrance, released by the showers, perfumed the moist air.

On a neighbour island, she waited patiently while a

golden retriever, dressed in a bow tie and plaid waistcoat, tail wagging, dragged a wagon bearing the wedding rings up to the ninth hole on the local mini-golf course, attended by a bride and groom wearing shorts and sports shirts while their two toddlers ran rampant on the green.

"It doesn't matter how they do the ceremony," the marriage commissioner told the Church Warden's wife. "It is basically all the same. It's about a public commitment." She observed that most of the brides were one to four years older than their grooms: "It is their biological clock ticking."

She added, "If most brides knew how they really looked in strapless dresses, with their bosoms bulging, they wouldn't wear them. No matter how small their breasts or what size dress they wear."

Fortunately, the cousin's wedding went off without a hitch. On cue, the sun emerged coyly from the clouds. Dogs raced in and out of the water and rolled in the debris along the surf line, shaking a stinking shower of seawater over the pants and skirts of some guests. A raven swooped overhead, squawking dire prophesies of martial storms ahead.

Seals popped their heads out of the water to stare at the wedding party like drive-by onlookers at a highway wreck and popped under the waves again. The guitar music was accompanied by the screams of playing children knee deep in the ocean slapping seawater at each other.

Finally the homemade vows were exchanged, the official blessings given, the bridal kisses bestowed. With a collective sigh of relief that the ceremony had concluded without incident beyond the odd twisted ankle and drenched clothes of the little cousins, the wedding party gathered for the wedding pictures.

The local photographer had been engaged to record the historic event. She posed her family groupings. The group shot of guests and the bridal party. The bridal party itself. Then the bridal couple, followed by the bride's family. The couple with the groom's family. The couple with distant relatives from distant places.

So far, so good, the photographer thought with relief as she moved discreetly among the guests, snapping pictures. Weddings tended to reveal family feuds, uncover buried tensions, emotions. She remembered the wedding with five grandfathers, all jostling for position among various configurations of children and stepchildren. Or the one where the bride refused to be pictured with her much younger stepmother. That family wedding portrait took some coaxing to produce.

Then there was the father-daughter, mother-son, sibling rivalry thing. One bride burst into tears and fled because her father didn't tell her she was beautiful in her wedding dress. One matron of honour, a sister, had a meltdown and didn't show up, leaving the photographer to park her camera and help dress the irate bride.

At one wedding the worried father told the photographer, "I feel as if I have forgotten something." She looked down at his bare feet. "Your shoes?" she prompted him.

She thought fondly of another wedding, where the adoptive family met the birth family of a bride for the first time and everyone got along splendidly, uplifted by the joyous event. That was fun to shoot, with the sunshine and music and the sea breeze teasing the pastel skirts of the bridesmaids.

The Church Warden and his wife waited expectantly on the sidelines, waiting for the call as the hosts to join the bridal party for the official pictures. Smoothly shaved, he had worn his navy jacket and freshly ironed shirt over his khaki pants, an agreeable change from his usual rumpled outfit. She had worn her floral print dress and her one string of pearls, her mousy hair pinned behind her ears.

This would be the finest picture of the two of them since their own wedding portrait, a picture for the family album, even, possibly destined to be posted by one of the cousins who knew the art of Facebook and YouTube on some future Ancestry.ca website.

"That's it!" cried the bride's father. "Time to head up to the bus for the ride to the wedding reception." He started herding the wedding guests, cautious in their heels and sandals, up the rocky path toward the parking lot at the top of the cliff where the school bus waited to take them back to the Community Hall and the menu of grilled salmon, potato salad, coleslaw, and apple and lemon meringue pie. Some things are a constant on the coast.

That's it? That's all? The wife stumbled in her heels across the rocky beach and grabbed the arm of the photographer who was starting to pack up her equipment. "But what about us?" she cried. The young photographer retrieved her arm and consulted a piece of paper that she pulled out of her camera bag. "You are not on the list," she said.

Not on the list! "But we're the hosts!" she wailed. The young photographer shrugged and moved away to continue dismantling and stowing her gear, eager to ensure she was not left behind on the beach.

The Warden's wife was stunned. Not on the list! There must be some mistake! She turned to seek support from the bridal couple but they were absorbed in transporting themselves and the bride's trailing train along the stony beach to the path.

The Warden snorted and turned away, pulling a round can of Copenhagen tobacco out of his front pants pocket, and selecting a plug that he placed in his cheek. He knew this habit irritated his wife, but it calmed him. He walked away from her. He didn't care to have his picture taken with his wife's relatives anyway.

His wife stayed on the beach, stiff with shock. She had trouble breathing. Beneath the print dress her chest was caught in a viselike grip of guilt. Who did she think she was? A member of the wedding party? She wasn't, was she? Merely the distant cousin and humble host. Her body burned with mortification. Above her on the cliff, her niece waved and called. "Come on, Aunty! We are going to your place first! We can't be late!"

She thought of the dill sauce chilling in the fridge. It must be spooned into bowls and set out on the tables in the Community Hall. The ice had to be added to the lemonade, the dog leashed. There were things to do to ensure the wedding dinner was a success. After all, it was a family wedding.

She owed it to her family! Didn't she?

STORM

SHE WOKE IN THE EARLY morning hours, the comfortable bulk of her husband, his back turned to her, exuding a familiar blend of heat, earthy body smells, and snuffled snores, and the white cat curled in the hillocks and humps of the bedding trenched between them.

She heard the wind rising and the rain falling, unknown objects plunking on the metal roof. Storm coming through, she thought. She opened one eye to check the clock, whose illuminated face showed the power was still on. The backup, windup alarm clock ticked. She slept.

Just before 5:25 AM she woke up and turned off the silent alarm before it could ring and wake her husband, but he had abandoned her and the cat to stretch out on the living room sofa, snoring peacefully, the TV remote in his hand, talking heads bobbing on a muted CNN channel. The cat curled up on the end of the bed, choosing the warm comfort of the house over its basement den when the rains came.

The house was cold. Outside the wind whipped the wet forest. She showered quickly and dressed. In the darkened kitchen she made a mug of tea to drink in the car, adding sugar and milk for extra strength—she normally drank it black—and toasted two thick pieces of bread from the local bakery that she spread with peanut butter, wrapped in a paper napkin, and put in her purse.

After writing a note reminding her husband to take out the compost, she shrugged into her all-weather parka, collected her tea mug, and eased into the car at 6:05 AM carrying a stack of newspapers to read on the ferry. She had loaded her bags the night before to simplify the early morning routine.

The ferry lineup was just outside their gate, cars and trucks crouching in the dark, their headlights gleaming like animal eyes in the rain. Rolling down the window of her Toyota hatchback, she asked the rain-slickered ticket agent, working her way up the ferry lineup with her ticket box, if the morning ferries were running.

No one at the terminal knew when she phoned at 5:00 AM, the ticket agent answered. Everyone was waiting for the marine radio's early morning forecast on wind and wave conditions in the Gulf separating the islands from the Mainland.

"You'll know more when you get to the ferry transfer port," she said, waving the travellers on board the inter-island vessel that had struggled down the storm-tossed channel and was snug in her island berth, landing lights shining, illuminating the wharf.

The transfer port separated the island travellers headed for the Mainland from those travelling on to the Big Island on board the inter-island ferry. She was going to the Mainland for a carefully orchestrated two-day agenda of physiotherapy for her sore back, medical appointments, errands, and lunch and dinner dates with friends. The round-trip fare was expensive, even with the seniors' discount, so every Mainland minute counted.

On board the inter-island ferry, most passengers huddled in the dark interiors of their cars rather than brave the rain-lashed deck to climb the stairs to the lighted cabin above deck with its stale coffee machine and hard metal chairs.

Over the almost inaudible loudspeaker, the captain announced that the mainline ferries between the Big Island and the Mainland were cancelled due to weather, but there was a fifty-fifty chance the smaller Gulf ferry to the Mainland would sail from the transfer port on the next island.

But when they arrived at the transfer point they learned that the Gulf ferry was cancelled too. The ferry system was a marine maze, the traveller thought, hard to navigate without a chart.

The Mainland drivers, including our traveller, decided to board the inter-island ferry to the Big Island and wait for the mainline ferries to resume sailing. After boarding the handful of trucks and cars in the blinding rain, the little ferry scuttled like a crab through the scudding waves in the dawn light to the next small island on its circuitous route.

The traveller dug out her cell phone and left messages on her doctor's office voice mail, cancelling her morning medical appointments. She then called her lunch date, whom she knew from long association was up at 6:30 AM each day.

"What are you doing out there? It's blowing 100 K in the Gulf," said her friend, a recreational sailor. They agreed to rebook lunch.

The passengers on the little ferry were a convivial group. They included a former islander and her American boyfriend, who were off to the west, west coast to watch the winter waves. The baker and his wife, more formally dressed than usual—if the men's shorts he wore year-round could ever be considered formal—were going to Convocation at the local university to attend their daughter's graduation from law school. The cancer patient, who was scheduled for a chemotherapy treatment, and her volunteer driver discussed how they could rebook two days of blood work and chemo. Everyone helped themselves to the stack of newspapers from the recycling bin.

The seas heaved and the islands were shrouded in rain fog.

When they arrived at the Big Island terminal hours later, the traveller drove first to the Mainland ticket booth, where the agent said ferries were still not running across the Gulf to the Mainland, and waved her back to the inter-island ferry lane to return to her home island that she had left three hours earlier.

Back on board, the homeward-bound passengers regrouped in the upper deck cabin on the little ferry and discussed the futility of ferry travel. But half an hour out from the terminal, in the protective lee of the first island on the sea route, the little ferry slowed down, the engines faltering, the wake churning in the white-capped waves. As the passengers on the upper deck watched with apprehension, the ferry slowly reversed.

"We are going back!" cried the cancer patient. "I have never seen that happen before!"

The captain announced over the loudspeaker that the wave conditions in the channel ahead were too rough and they were returning to the Big Island port. The passengers sat at their tables, glumly sipping the sour coffee from the machine as the little ferry bucked her way back through the pelting rain and foaming seas to a safe harbour.

Back on land, the traveller drove through the Mainland ticket booth again where the agent confirmed the Gulf ferries were still cancelled and the ships remained marooned at their docks. The waiting cars were lined up in alternative lanes, creating an unusual pattern in the ferry parking lot. "Park in lane 12," the agent said. "That way if you decide to leave you can pull out of the lineup."

The traveller parked her car and scurried through the wind and rain to the warmth of the coffee shop where she ordered herb tea and a cinnamon bun. She sat down at a table beside two women leafing through fashion magazines. They were discussing what movies they should see on their visit to the city.

In time-honoured ferry tradition, the traveller joined the conversation uninvited and suggested her personal choice. "It is worth seeing for the clothes and the food," she offered. The women discussed the virtues of Meryl Streep and Julia Roberts as they waited for the loudspeaker announcement that finally confirmed both the 11:00 AM and 1:00 PM sailings were cancelled.

"Time to go home," said the two women, collecting their purses. They lived on the Big Island and could at least return to their homes. Not so the inter-island travellers.

Returning to her car, sloshing over the rain-drenched parking lot, the traveller drove slowly through the storm to the nearest shopping mall, careful to avoid hydroplaning on the water-slicked highway, and parked by a bookstore where she found a paperback version of a new novel and a collection of Sudoku puzzles for her husband's birthday.

The bookstore founder, a long-time Liberal, walked her out the door of the bookstore and through the rain, steadying her elbow as the wind gusted, and deposited her in front of the candy shop, as he asked her who would win the Liberal leadership race.

"I am just being polite," he said. He knew she wasn't a Liberal. The couple voted Green or NDP. She told him his candidate would lose. "I expect so," sighed the bookseller, turning up the collar of his rain slicker.

In the candy shop, with great deliberation and ignoring her diet regimen, she chose her favourite comfort food, 100 grams of chocolate-covered ginger. When she had eaten every piece, she left the candy shop and made her way down the mall to a men's store and bought a shirt for her husband.

The storm squalled through the main street, slapping the glass storefronts with fistfuls of water. At the end of the street the angry seas furiously whipped the white-capped waves, faster, faster, until they collapsed on the stony beach.

By now she was thoroughly cold and wet. The rain pooled in her hoodie and when she pulled it up over her head, water drenched her hair and face. Miserable, slashed by the wind and rain, she returned to the candy store that doubled as a café and sat at a table by the front window. She knew her close friends, who had moved off island, usually had coffee there on weekday mornings.

Her friends saw her through the window and splashed their way inside, droplets flying from their umbrella. "*There you are,*" they cried, as if they had planned to meet. Over coffee they traded gossip and family news.

From time to time other ferry refugees came into the shop to report on the ferry situation. Her friends volunteered spare beds and supper if the ferries didn't sail that night.

After waving her friends goodbye she made her way through the gusts to the supermarket where she bought a pot roast in a bag, some instant scalloped potatoes, and a purple eggplant—her husband's favourite vegetable, not usually available on island. Next she managed to make it to the hardware store where she bought a new flashlight and a windup emergency radio. Then she sloshed through the street to her car and drove back to the terminal.

Sitting in her car with the other stranded vehicles, immobilized in the rain, she experienced a curious sense of suspended time and purpose, almost an out-of-body experience. She decided she would take whatever ferry left first, for wherever it was going. She might disappear entirely, like the woman in the Alice Munro story who left her kitchen and boarded the mid-island ferry and vanished forever.

Then she thought of her husband and cat, and with resignation and guilt she started her car and drove over to the inter-island ferry lineup. Miraculously, she heard the loudspeaker announce that the inter-island ferry was in the terminal and that all passengers were to return to their vehicles in preparation for boarding. Amazingly, despite the waves and the mist and the weather, the ferry left port on schedule in the rain-dark afternoon.

When the ferry rounded the point and headed down the channel for her home island, and after the ferry passed the mid-channel marker, the boundary of cell phone reception, she phoned her husband to tell him that she was coming home.

"I wouldn't advise that," he replied, concerned. "The power is out on island."

She peered through the rain. No lights shone anywhere on the timbered shores lining the channel.

"I don't have an alternative," she cried, thinking of the woman in the Alice Munro story who obviously did. When the ferry docked she drove the short distance to her darkened house and threw the newspapers into the recycling bin in the carport. She had spent ten hours on four ferries, going nowhere.

Outside the front door there was a wheelbarrow filled with wood for the wood stove. Inside she found her husband sitting at the dining room table, trying to do a puzzle in the dim light of a battery-powered lamp.

The wood stove warmed the house. She pulled out her new flashlight and windup radio and gave them to her husband who immediately wound up the radio and tried to find a news station through the static.

She found the emergency bag in the hall cupboard and pulled out the old emergency flashlight, which worked, and the old emergency radio that didn't. She put the pot roast into a casserole dish, stirred water and milk into the scalloped potatoes and put them in the wood stove oven, pushing them to the back of the oven rack.

She sliced the eggplant with onions and tomatoes and a squirt of lemon juice and put the pan in the front of the oven. She stoked the stove and added wood. She fed the white cat a salmon-flavoured Tender Treat. I am beginning to learn the ropes of island life, she thought.

When she had done all that the smoke alarm chirped and the power came back on.

They spent the evening eating pot roast and watching television reports: Havoc on the Mainland, Two Hundred Thousand without Hydro. Flooding Creeks. Power Lines Down, Fallen Trees Block Roads. Highways Closed, Trucks Stranded.

Outside the brightly lit warm little house the wind moaned in the rainforest.

That night she woke to silence. No wind, no rain. Only the sound of the purring cat from the end of the bed.

She slept.

THE INLET

THE VILLAGE IS PICTURE PERFECT. The small, spare homes are stitched in a crazy quilt pattern bordered by a boardwalk along the foreshore of the Inlet just before it empties into the larger Sound. There is no road to the village. A logging road through the forest ends at the opposite shore, where the school and Community Hall stand among the trees, but access between the two settlements is by boat.

Early morning fog normally veils the village and the dark green water hemming the shoreline. Sunshine pierces the fog, like spears from the Great Spirit, revered by residents of the Indian reserve at the head of the Inlet. Eagles drift through the shafts of sunlight. Bear paws fresco the freshly poured cement walk of one home. The damage done by bears to village vegetable gardens and berry bushes is a common complaint.

The village reality is not so pretty. The salmon run has dwindled, idling the fishboats tied up to the government dock. No fish means no fish in the smokehouses of the Indian reserve, a food staple for its residents. An abandoned fish cannery collapses against the shore. The community school is in danger of closing for lack of pupils as families pack up and move out in search of jobs.

Decaying buildings lurch toward the ground, victims of money laundering by the drug dealers who smuggle their goods from the open Pacific beyond the Sound, out of sight of the law, if not the keepers of the local light station.

Raw sewage filters from the ancient septic tanks through the gravel beaches into the sea. There are not enough tax-payers to finance the waste-water management systems demanded by municipal governments. There is, in fact, no municipal government.

It seems like the whole village is for sale.

Into this landscape arrives the author, her SUV shrouded with the dust from the main haul logging roads she drove from nearby Port. She dreams of a literary festival rooted in the village. Readings by famous authors. Workshops for creative writing students.

She takes over the dilapidated Community Hall for this purpose. She is partly successful, attracting some American boaters and a few tourists who brave the logging road from Port to camp in the trees of the nearby provincial park and swim in the open ocean.

The festival authors love the West Coast setting and the chance to meet one another over drinks in the local pub or at a community salmon barbeque, as the setting sun sinks into a streak of clouds above the ocean. They love watching some of the gillnet fishing fleet, their holds filled with sockeye, weave ribbons of wake through the wind-ruffled water as they head for the dock, their running lights twinkling in the gloom—red for port, green for starboard.

The locals can't afford to go to the literary events, but they are willing volunteers, transporting visitors back and forth across the Inlet in their outboards to the bed and breakfast hosts, and selling wine and coffee and biscotti, the festival's only apparent revenue source beyond the slim ticket sales.

The author has been attracted to the village by the local contract logger, a Malcolm Lowry type who logs mostly in the rain that runs down the steel spar tree and along the cables that drag the dripping logs over the soaked forest floor to the logging trucks, marooned in the puddles of the gravel haul road. The logs are loaded and hauled to the log dump and tipped into the sea.

The logger has amused himself during forest closures, for fire in summer and snow in winter, by writing a lusty, brawling novel, *The Gyppo Logger Blues*, about the days of the hand-loggers who first attacked the forests sloping down the Inlet mountains with their axes and handsaws.

The regional media, sick of the box-store discount discards of books by unknown American authors, adores

The Gyppo Logger Blues. So do readers. All those hard hats and plaid shirts and caulked boots and whisky binges in the bunkhouses of the coast plastered with pictures of near-naked women.

The logger knows his income is secured by the fact that the town-based owner of the timber licence has no logging skills and cannot do any of the jobs in camp or in the bush, and thus depends on the logger to provide his income. The logger can afford time off.

The logger meets the author at a writer's festival on the other coast where she fishes for literary fodder for her own books. They team up for readings in the regional schools and literacy programs sponsored by the regional newspapers.

Sometime, someplace, bonded by the communal culture of the literary arts, they begin an affair.

The logger's wife knows this. She is a striking-looking woman with the dark hair of a tribal ancestor and the blue eyes of her Finnish father, a fisherman based in the Inlet. She and her parents lived on the fishboat, gutting and cleaning the fish until their hands were swollen, cooking on the gas stove in the galley below deck, and sleeping in bunk beds in the forward cabin. In winter she attended school in Port, boarding with her aunt.

She met her logger at a Loggers Sports Day dance when she was seventeen years old. After the wedding they returned to the Inlet where they live in a former float home dragged ashore in the cove across the Sound from the village. She digs kelp into her vegetable garden and knits sweaters, mitts, and scarves for her husband and young children, a boy and a girl.

The converted float house is small but snug. She likes to sit in her rocking chair by the window where she can see the boom boats skidding over the water, sorting the logs into flat rafts in the booming grounds in the cove, preparing them for the long tow to the mills on the other coast.

She likes to see the sun polish the band of yellow cedar that threads the darker hemlock forest across the cove. She likes to see an eagle plummet like a stone, hitting the sea and emerging with a surprised salmon in its claws. She also sees the logger and his lover, laughing and lacquered with lust as they climb in and out of the float planes that roar back and forth from Port to the camp.

All this she sees from her window.

She does not feel particularly threatened by the affair. The author is unlikely to leave her hippie-type attic apartment and her writer's convivial, wine-lubricated discussion groups to move to the bush. She also knows her husband. It is not his first affair. There had been the teacher. Then the visiting nurse. She is unsure about the wife of the fish plant operator.

She doesn't much mind the affair. What she objects to is its public nature, displayed to audiences up and down the coast, in lavish dining rooms and wine bars while she sips tea at home. She wants revenge.

She rocks. She knits. She plans it.

There is a hierarchy of status in a logging camp as stringent as any Victorian class system with its lords and ladies and forelock-tugging peasants. The logging operator, usually also the owner, and his wife reign over the camp. If camp is large enough, there is the forest engineer who designs the roads system and logging plan and log dump.

The high riggers are the kings of the woods, climbing the tallest tree in a logging show by digging their spurred caulk boots into the ribbed, rope-like bark and hauling themselves up the hemlock or fir or spruce tree with their belts, climbing as they go.

Their equal are the fallers, who plough into the dense underbrush to select and notch the tree with their chainsaws to that exquisite point where it will crack and fall heavily into the bush exactly where the faller plans to lay it. An error can cause death. Too many still die in the woods.

The thump of a felled giant, quaking the earth where it lands, is a very satisfactory sound on a sunny morning in the inland forests of the Inlet.

The hierarchy ladders its way down to the bullbuckers, who buck the fallen timber into logs, and grapple operators who load them into the trucks, engines panting, with drivers that screech their way down the switchbacks, pumping brakes, to the log dump. The splash of a load of logs, spouting spumes of water where they hit the sea, is also a satisfactory sound on a sunny morning in the Inlet.

The lowest man on the logging crew is the chokerman,

who hauls the choker cables from the spar tree through the snarled, savage underbrush, up and over fallen logs entrapped in the tangle of bushes and berries and small saplings growing out of their bark. He wrangles the chokers around the bucked log so it can be hauled to the landing. Hot, sweaty, sticky work in rain or in shine, bitten by mosquitoes, slashed by nettles.

The logger's wife chooses the senior chokerman in camp. He is small and bandy legged, useful in his line of work, with pale blue eyes and a twitching nose, silent to the point of muteness. A rabbit of a man with nothing to recommend him except his status as a non-entity.

His partner is a tall, voluptuous woman with freckles and rusty hair, who runs the camp cookhouse. The couple has no children. The contract logger's wife has caught the chokerman's woman eying the logger with the speculative scrutiny that a horse breeder might employ to assess a potential stud horse.

The logger's wife invites the chokerman's woman to tea in the converted float house. Sitting in her rocking chair by the window, serving blueberry muffins and tea with canned Pacific milk, she proposes a spouse swap to her guest. The chokerman's woman is startled. But she does not reject the proposal.

Both wives can anticipate the possibilities, the problems. The spouse swap cannot take place in camp. That would upset the balance between the boss and the crew, and the social status of the wives. However it is negotiated, it still must be accepted by their husbands. That proves the lesser task.

The author, when she later learns this, does not of course know what was actually said in that living room, how the proposal was presented, the way it was received, whether the response was eager or demure. Nothing in her fictional world, with its romantic wraiths of dialogue, sly flirtations, and passionate declarations of love, can produce a coherent precedent.

Whenever she thinks of the scene, which is often, her mind goes as blank as ocean fog. She learns of the swap from the logger himself, on one of their liaisons in town at the airport hotel that serves as a meeting place for the two lovers between book festivals and workshops.

Wrapped in a frayed hotel sheet damp with post-coital sweat and stained with his semen, he describes how the two couples planned a cross-border trip to a gambling casino, the tension at the border when the American customs officials examined their passports, the suspense of checking into the casino hotel with another man's wife or the other wife's husband, the sheer excitement of pairing off with their new partners and heading for the elevators, pretending not to look at each other and vanishing behind impersonal doors, to re-emerge later to dine communally and to shoot craps or hit the blackjack tables with the non-chalance of strangers.

Listening to all this, one ear cocked for the housekeeper's door knock since it is check-out time, the author finds herself swirling between whirlpools of prurient fascination (then what happened, tell me more) and of gut-wrenching nausea (stop, shut up, this is making me sick) all the while recording, in some inner space, what she is feeling to recycle later in her fiction.

She cannot drag herself off the connubial bed to distance herself from her lover. Instead she sits numbly among the sheets, while he recounts with shining eyes and the occasional chuckle his amorous adventures.

Caught up in his drama, the logger seems oblivious to her. She comes to see that he feels whatever else has altered in his world, their position has not changed. He might substitute another man's wife for his own, but his mistress is a constant.

When she realizes that, she climbs off the bed and pukes in the toilet. She grabs her clothes and leaves, to his amazement. What is wrong with *her*?

In the weeks and months that follow she notes impersonally that she feels frozen, blue-ice cold, immune to feelings or thoughts or even guilt. She does not want to die but she does not care if she lives. She records her reactions in her journal for use in the future. The very distant future.

She does not see her logger. Instead she sees his wife, who phones the author in her attic apartment the following spring and invites her for lunch. This has never happened in the past.

Despite her reservations, actually, her stomach-churning revulsion at the sound of the wife's voice, out of sheer curiosity the author accepts. They meet on neutral ground, the terrace of a downtown café near the bus station that neither has visited before.

Over seafood salad and iced tea, the wife recounts distantly, as if commenting on an event that is taking place on another continent or which she has read about or has watched on television, that she and her chokerman have decided to leave their spouses and become life partners in a valley town. The children will go with them.

The logger and his redheaded woman, which is what the logging crew calls her, will stay on in camp.

The author is too dazed to take this all in at once. She chews her prawns and swallows her tea, allowing the ice cubes to mute her cold lips. She murmurs condolences and congratulations and feigns expressions of concern. They split the bill and say their cool, cordial goodbyes.

After they leave the café, the wife walks to the bus station and the author heads for her attic, where she lies on her back on the plaid-covered box spring and probes her reactions, taking her emotional pulse so she can write them down. For use in that distant future.

The camp's close-knit community is irreparably destroyed. When the local timber licence is cut over, the camp moves and the logger and his woman move with it. The few other women in camp, uncomfortable with the bunkhouse gossip, discuss their children's need for a broader education and leave for the Port's sprawling suburbs. The abandoned log dump and booming grounds become, briefly, a fish farm that later goes bankrupt.

Across the Sound in the village on the Inlet, the literary festival fades away, like so many coastal dreams. The tides come in and the tides go out, leaving the beaches festooned with necklaces of thick, dark kelp decorated with broken shells. The cries of the ospreys and gulls compete with the thud of the ocean surf beyond.

Years later the author runs into her logger in a hotel lobby in town. He is balding, weathered, crippled with arthritis, but his gaze is still fond as he looks at her. She wonders what she ever saw in him. Then, years later still, she meets his son, who has the same loose-limbed, muscled body, the same eyes. He hugs her, and her body remembers.

The author never comes back to the village. Over beers in the wharf pub, some say she went east.

SEA WOLF

Two sheep are dead and five wounded after an attack by a dog or wolf on island. The Animal Control Officer verified it was indeed the work of a dog, but surveyors working nearby described the animal as agitated, dark but not solid coloured, heavy coated like a wolf, possibly a Malamute/ Alsatian/Husky mix with blue eyes. The animal was later seen attacking cats in the cove.

—Undated clipping from the local *Salish Sounder* newspaper

THE EDITOR OF THE COASTAL community newspaper sat at the corner table in the wharf pub, sipping a Race Rocks beer and thumbing through his notebook. He was waiting for the ferry, keeping an eye on the empty channel beyond the pub window, watching for the ship to poke its bow around the point of the neighbouring island. The captain's chair was hard on his middle-aged butt.

He was on island revisiting a story he had written years ago as a young reporter about a predator animal that invaded the island, ensnaring the islanders' imaginations, creating anxiety in some and anticipation in others, branded deep into the islanders' collective memory.

Then, his hopes for a national journalistic career were pure, untarnished by the reality of the job market. He eventually settled into the editor/circulation/advertising manager roles of a small regional weekly.

He became aware over the years that every community on the coast had its own animal story—the cougar snarling in the kitchen, the black bear feasting in the blackberry patch, the wolf loping through the woods—stories that became implanted in coastal myths from Aboriginal times to the present day.

Why? he wondered. What was it about these animal images that shaped and stained each community's history and mystique over decades, centuries, since time beyond memory? It certainly wasn't consistency. Nobody he interviewed told the same story. He would never again believe an eyewitness account.

Ordering another beer, he reviewed his interview with the musician, which took place over coffee in the General Store café. A veteran of the days before tape recorders were allowed into courtrooms, he took down statements in a swift but accurate scribble only he could decipher.

"It snowed the winter the wolf came. I can't remember the year. The schoolteacher and I were talking about the wolf during the goat count up on the ridge last week, how there were no predators to cull the herd since they killed the wolf," she told him. "When was that? Ten years ago? Fifteen? The schoolteacher said she has a photo of her daughter with the wolf's body on the wharf. Her daughter was a toddler then. She would be this high—no, maybe that high." The musician measured the distance from the café floor with her hand.

"Well, she's a teenager now," she continued. "We should look for the photo in the local newspaper. Maybe it would show the date. Funny how I can't remember the year. But I remember the snow. It was a wolf. Some people said it was a dog. Someone else said it was half dog, half wolf. If it was a dog, the sheep farmers could have been compensated for their losses. Not so if sheep were killed by wild animals.

"Where did it come from? Probably swam over from another island. No, I think it was brought here. Remember that couple that came for a few months from the Big Island with a puppy like a German shepherd? It vanished, left behind when they moved. Nobody really knows."

The bartender brought the beer to the table. Thanking him, the editor turned the pages of his steno pad to the next interview, with the local mechanic in the garage behind the store.

"It wasn't a dog or a half dog. It was a Sea wolf," the mechanic said, carefully salvaging a wheel from a crumpled truck. "Short and squat, with a big chest, massive front paws, like a Great Dane, but there are no Great Danes on island. It had a big canine head, a tapered body.

"They say the route of the Sea wolf starts across the border, winds up through coastal mountains to the Interior, down through the coastal inlets to the mid coast, then over to the Big Island. Some of them probably swam over to the islands, swimming from island to island.

"Sea wolves are great swimmers. They follow the deer hunting route. Fast. They can travel fifty to seventy kilometres in an evening. A wolf is a real running machine.

"You think a Sea wolf is an Aboriginal myth? Nah, Sea wolves are real. Different from the Timber wolf, which is tall, thin and lean, built for moving through snow and timber.

"Remember that story about the islander who outran a wolf through the snow in Yukon? That guy must have been in great shape. Of course he was a young man then.

"Are they still around? I don't know. Ours was here almost a year. Maybe two years. It would have been fine if it just killed the deer and the feral goats. After it came there were dead deer all over the place. The wolf would rip open the carcass, take the heart and the liver, and leave the rest.

"But it started killing the sheep on the farm. It killed eight sheep. No, two sheep. No, five sheep that winter. The others the next year. The farmer was worried because he couldn't pen the sheep for the night to protect them from the wolf. And it killed the llama that must have weighed 300 pounds.

The llama was defending the sheep. Some people say the llama liked to hike to the ferry dock to meet the visitors. But that is ridiculous. I never saw it at the dock!"

The mechanic finished working on the truck and wiped his hands on his oil-stained overalls.

The editor turned in his chair to check the empty channel. He turned back to his notes on the mountain man, whom he had tracked to his lair high on the cliffs.

"I know people were afraid of the wolf. But I liked it being here. It knocked down the feral goats. They are killing the island, those goats. The old bachelor goats use those horns to beat the heck out of the trees. Those horns will turn the bark into mush, which the goats eat. That kills the trees. That's why I encourage hunters to shoot goats on my land. The Greeks used to come to shoot the kid goats for Easter dinner. They don't come so much anymore.

"I have killed more than 200 goats over the years. You say this year's goat count was 262 goats? So I have killed almost half the original herd? I am not proud of it. But those goats, they turn those trees into pulp. They eat the young trees. They tear out the Garry oak, the young Douglas fir. Soon there will be no trees left. We will lose the cliffs. They will turn into rock. No timbered ridges on the cliff. It will be like the Greek islands. Just rock. Those goats will leave the island completely naked.

"Then we will lose the golden eagles. We have five golden eagles on island. We are the only island with golden eagles.

You heard them screeching in the trees when I took you out in my boat. No, I won't tell you where they nest. No one will. People will go looking for them.

"The eagles kill the goats. An eagle will try and knock a goat off the ridge, so it will hurt itself. The eagle will swoop down on the goat's head and put its claws through the goat's eyeballs.

"The eagle is the only creature that will take on a wolf. An eagle will punch-hit a wolf, try to slow it down, then dig its claws into the jawbone of the wolf to sever the jugular vein in the throat.

"Why has the story of the wolf taken such a hold on island? I dunno. I think people like to have something scary out there. It's a bonding thing. People would form hunting parties to go out after the wolf. Protecting ourselves from something.

"At night it was out there. Somewhere out there was something in the dark that could kill us."

Fear was a common thread in the tapestry of island memories. Memory and myth. Ordering a side of yammies from the bored bartender, the editor next read a local poet's views.

"I saw the wolf tracks on the road winding up through the forest. How did I know they were wolf tracks? They were the size of a fist. And the game people had marked the tracks with tiny flags to show where it had come and gone. Probably tracking Salvador Dali Llama. That is what some people called the llama, who was found dead. You say the llama was killed on the other side of the island? I dunno, but Salvador Dali often climbed up the hill on the road. People saw him peeking into their windows.

"You think the wolf was maybe 150 pounds? No. I saw it on the wharf, dead. It was smaller than that. It was quite a young animal. It could have lived a long life if it had stuck to killing goats and deer.

"Did I ever see the wolf alive? No, but as I walked up the road I felt the possibility it was watching me. It may or may not be. Couldn't be sure. I was aware that we ourselves were prey. I wrote a poem about it. I think we have a genetic memory of being prey. A genetic memory of when the world was full of menace.

"Everyone was afraid that the next victim would be a child. And for the sheep farm there was the threat to its livelihood. That family depends on the income from the sheep.

"Why were people so fearful? This is a benign environment, and suddenly there was this sense of menace. A sense of mass hysteria swept around the island. People wrote about the wolf in the local newspaper, describing it as an agent of the Devil.

"It was a wolf, for God's sake, doing what wolves do!"

The editor drank his beer and rubbed his forehead with his hand. Red eyes or blue eyes. Maybe a huge animal or possibly a small one. Dog, wolf, or half wolf, half dog. He turned to the report of the volunteer librarian, whom he interviewed at her desk as she methodically sorted and stamped a pile of returned books.

"No, I never saw the wolf. I saw its footprints, very clear in the mud, larger than those of a dog, as big as my hand. I knew it was a wolf, right in my bones. Scared? I was kind of excited, kind of thrilled, also a little fearful. The wolf was near. What if it was here? It made us on guard when we went walking in the woods. It was a new feeling. It gave us courage.

"After it was dead, I found out it was small. That picture of it on the dock, it looked like a dog. It wasn't big at all. He became like a fairy tale, a huge wolf with red eyes. It did kill the llama, a strange creature with a long neck.

"Then it got to where it killed someone's dog, a golden retriever. I had a golden. Nice dogs. It was tied up, put out there like putting a goat for the lion. The dog didn't have a chance.

"That's when I began to turn against the wolf.

"The reality was it was a young wolf, without a pack. It never learned to hunt, so it did these clumsy killings. It was on its own. A lone wolf, trying to make its way. People— especially women—romanticize the idea of the lone wolf, someone who lives outside the borders of society.

"It was a young wolf that was trying to survive and didn't know how to do it very well. There is sadness to it, a kind of pathos. After all this big buildup, it was an ordinary animal, lying dead on the dock." The librarian was thoughtful as she picked up the next book.

Today he saw that the ferry was rounding the point on the island farther down the channel. It would take twenty-five minutes to dock. The door to the pub banged open and the pub lunch crowd blew in.

They placed their lamb burger and salmon burger orders with the bartender, picked up their beers, and came over to the round corner table to join the editor, who knew them from his previous visits. Fingering his pen, he asked them whether they were on island when the wolf ran rampant.

"Yeah, I remember when it killed the llama," said one man as he hung his bomber jacket over the back of his chair and sat down. "The game officers came over and set traps around the sheep pastures. You could see them sneaking through the woods in their uniforms. But they never caught the predator.

"The wolf killed deer all over the place, it killed raccoons—we found bits and pieces all over the beaches. It killed all the baby goats that year. Gobbled up all the babies. You could see the tiny hooves in the wolf scat. And there were the dead cats. Only bits of cat hair left mixed up with the dead leaves on the forest floor.

"The wolf killed by attacking from behind, clamping big canine teeth on the back of the neck, snapping the spine. It killed that big red setter out at the Point. It was alone. When it killed a deer, it tore it open and ate the heart, the liver, and the rump.

"Most wolves travel in packs, and when the alpha male has eaten the choice bits, he shares it with the pack. But this wolf was alone. And all that protein—it was a problem—like being on steroids, made it aggressive. People feared for their children.

"Did anyone actually see it? Just glimpses. My neighbour saw it once on the road. He went down the road in the snow and there were no wolf tracks. When he returned, wolf tracks crossed his human tracks. Must have hidden in the timber and watched him go down the road, and then crossed over. Makes a man shiver." He attacked his lamb burger.

"Well, I live alone up the mountain and I knew when the wolf was around," said the trucker, draining his pint of draft beer. "My dog would growl, go the door, listen, growl again, return to its bed beside the wood stove. Or get up and growl in the middle of the night, hairs stiff on its back.

"The caretaker on the next island shot the wolf. It was killing the sheep. They were drowning, jumping into the water, trying to escape the wolf. The caretaker killed the wolf at the Pass. It was trying to cross to south island. He used a rifle. What kind? Can't tell you. We are not supposed to use rifles, unless you're Aboriginal. He brought it over to the wharf. Looked like a dog. Big head. Must have weighed ninety pounds. I went down to the wharf to see it myself."

"I never saw it before it was shot," said a long-time resident and volunteer fireman. "But I saw the scat. I knew it was around. How big? Maybe eighty-five pounds. I think it was quite young. The game people came after it was shot and called it a Brindle wolf. They did DNA tests on it and said it was pure wolf. I think they did the tests because if it was part dog the sheep farmer would get compensation, but not if it was a wild animal. Or maybe it is the other way around.

"How did it get here? Maybe it swam. Or maybe someone brought it as a pup and when it got too hard to handle they released it into the forest.

"What amazed me was the size of the territory it covered and how far it could travel in a day and a night. You ask if it lived in the marsh. I don't think it lived anywhere. It roamed the islands. It should have stuck to killing deer. But it killed the goats, the dog, the llama, Salvador Dali, everybody's pet. That llama. It would peer down its nose at you, sneering. People wondered what the wolf would attack next." He pushed back his chair and went to the men's room.

When they had finished their meal, the pub lunch crowd paid their tabs, gave the editor a thumbs-up and left, banging the door behind them.

It was amazing how willing people were to share their memories of the Sea wolf. The editor had arranged to talk to the ferry terminal manager on the ferry as she returned home from town when he travelled to the island.

"I don't know what year the wolf came, but I was there when it was shot," she told him as they drank muddy coffee from the machine in the ship's dreary passenger lounge. "Well, not actually at the site but on a small boat off in the Pass.

"The caretaker's wife had looked out the window and saw the wolf running across the pasture. The caretaker called my son—the men had agreed that they would hunt for it in a group—and he took his gun and left.

"I went out to the Pass to watch for the wolf and saw the caretaker's wife in a small boat, with a gun lying on the bottom.

"'I have a gun,' she called out to me. 'Well, I have a cell phone,' I called back. So she brought the boat to shore and I hopped in with my cell so we could call if we saw the wolf. She said her job was to shoot the wolf if it came into the water.

"What kind of a gun? Don't know. Maybe a .22 rifle. Yeah, I know. Pretty hard to hurt a wolf with a .22, particularly when you're steering the boat too. Maybe her job was to shoot to let the men know the wolf was in the water. You should ask her if you can find her. They moved off island a few years ago.

"Anyway, we heard the shot that killed it. We landed the boat and went up to the house. What happened was the men were conducting a sweep of the pasture and the wolf got behind them and the caretaker shot it. You should ask my son—he was there. It was dead when I saw it in the back of the truck when they drove up to the house.

"The look on those guys' faces—except for the caretaker. They were so disappointed. Everyone wanted to be The One who shot it."

The editor had come across the caretaker and his wife quite by accident in the parking lot at the food co-op in town a few days earlier. In fact, this unexpected encounter had seeded his interest in following up the old story of the Sea wolf.

He hadn't seen them in years, and there they were, sitting in the cab of their Toyota Tacoma in the next parking slip. They walked over to the main street bakery, collected coffee and cinnamon buns, and sat down at a table to catch up.

The editor took his pen out of his jacket pocket and opened his notepad. "Tell me the story of the island wolf," he said, uncapping his pen. "Why did you kill it? Why not let it live?"

"Why?" said the caretaker, emptying two packets of sugar into his coffee. "Because he killed eight of my twelve sheep. It was playing with them, running along the cliffs, running them off the island. I found them in weird places. One sheep was found on the reef in the bay. It had to swim there. Wolf was a good swimmer, roaming from island to island.

"The wife went for a walk along the cliff. A flock of gulls attracted her to the cliff overlooking the Bay. There was a fresh killed sheep on the beach. Heart ripped out of its chest. So I decided: 'Let's go get him.' I got on the phone and rounded up the Posse. The sheep farmer called the cops. They called me on the phone and said, 'We'll be over.'"

The caretaker thrust his head across the table at the editor, challenging him. "We told the police, 'We don't want you.'"

The editor knew why. "Because your guns were not registered?"

The caretaker nodded. "Every member of the Posse had a gun but one. None was registered.

"The Wildlife guys came over a few weeks earlier but they couldn't find the wolf. We showed them the tracks. 'Yes, a wolf,' they said. Couldn't be anything else. They went out with the Posse but we had no guns. Waste of time. They were the only ones who could legally use guns. Nobody else could shoot. And those guys couldn't find the wolf.

"The RCMP understood. 'Keep us apprised,' they said. And we did. They met us on the dock when we took the body over."

"How did you catch him?" asked the editor, scribbling away in his notebook.

"We set up a push, a sweep to the cove," said the caretaker, drawing an imaginary map on the table top. "The Posse had men on the ridge, at the edge of the meadow. I was in the woods. The wolf came off the brow of the hill. He was going to his bed on the ridge.

"Two members of the Posse ran by—they didn't see him—but the wolf turned back to avoid them. I shot him in the heart under the shoulder." The caretaker turned his body and exposed his armpit to show the editor.

"He was running on a slant as he climbed back up the ridge," he continued. "I was at the right place at the right time, maybe 200 feet away. My gun? It was a 30.30 bush gun. No, it wasn't registered.

"Everybody came down the ridge to look at the wolf, to

take pictures. We put it in the truck, drove back to the house."

"It was very beautiful," said the wife. "It was grey, black, blond, white. Wolf colours to blend into the forest." She was a quiet woman, a quilter, who had missed the company of women on her isolated island. "The wolf had people bamboozled. You woke up at night and would hear it run by. Wondered what was that? People were afraid to go for a walk."

"Yes, it was sad, but I did what had to be done," said her husband. "A farmer looking after his critters. Not everybody felt that way. Police met us on the south island dock and took it away. Never saw it again.

"The sheep farmer who lost the most sheep promised $1000 to the shooter. Maybe price of three or four sheep. There was a big party at the pub to distribute the money to the Posse. I got maybe $300."

They were done. They walked back to their vehicles in the co-op parking lot and said goodbye.

The editor took the ferry to the island a few days later.

Now the ferry was nosing into the docking slip. The editor closed his notebook and paid his own bill at the bar.

"Why do so many islanders remember the wolf?" he asked the bartender, who had been listening to the stories as he polished the beer glasses and hung them on the rack over the bar.

The bartender considered his answer. "Why is it so much a part of our island history? I think it was because it is so rare that something happens on our island. Like when the cougar was seen at the Point. They think it came across on a log boom from the Big Island.

"The cougar?"

"The store manager shot it years ago. You remember, he kept the head in his freezer for four years. When he bought the store he hung the cougar head above the cash register. You should ask the Old Man about it. He'll tell you a tall tale or two. It was before my time, but we've all heard the story." He placed the last beer glass on the overhead rack and disappeared into the kitchen.

The editor pocketed his notebook and boarded the ferry. The islanders' differing accounts may not add up, he thought, but they certainly made a good story. And, with a nod to American poet Robert Frost, that made all the difference.

ACKNOWLEDGEMENTS

Our mother made rag rugs out of much-loved garments. We kids would search for treasures such as scraps from Father's old pyjamas, or a favourite blouse handed down by a beloved cousin. This book is essentially a literary rag rug woven from coastal memories, myths, and images collected over decades of working, travelling, and living on the BC coast.

Sailing the coastal channels with my twin, Jim. The wistful look on the face of a long-legged girl pumping diesel on a mid-coast fuel dock. Fishing for prawns and crabs with my daughter Jane and her husband Malcolm. Amazing sightings of orcas and other sea life on whale-watching tours. Visits to abandoned Aboriginal villages.

Flying the BC coast with foresters, log buyers, and Canadian Coast Guard officials in everything on floats, including a Twin Otter piloted by my son John. Flying headland to headland over the Pacific Ocean is a sublime experience.

Listening to stories in the cook houses of logging camps during my journalism years when I wrote for Vancouver newspapers and *The Truck Logger* magazine. Brave deeds recounted in lighthouse kitchens. Island stories about islanders.

People shared their own stories for this book. The late Rev. Sheila Flynn described life on the water as a Canadian Coast Guard Auxiliary volunteer. Don Dixon, Althea Rasmussen, and Rick Jones explained how tidewater communities are saving our cherished salmon runs. Al Stonehouse taught me the intricacies of growing garlic. Nancy Hendry contributed her medical expertise as a nurse practitioner. Jane Dixon-Warren outlined the duties of a provincial marriage commissioner. Retired fire chief John Wiznuk provided technical advice on dock fires. Juliet Kershaw gave me editing advice.

Every community has a wild animal story. Special thanks to my fellow Saturna islanders whose recollections, in their own words, contributed to "Sea Wolf." They include, in no particular order: Nancy Angermeyer, Geri Crooks, Ellen McGinn, Ilio Bertolami, Jeannie McLean, Mike and Debbie Graham, Jillian Tebbitt and the late Jean Paul Duplessis.

Finally, thanks to my "agent emeritus" Perry Goldsmith, who came out of retirement to find the right publisher, my long-time assistant and muse Janice McAdam, affable editor Renée Layberry, ever-patient publisher Taryn Boyd, and artist Bev Byerley, whose illustrations enliven the stories. Thanks as well to many others, whoever and wherever you are!